30p 50p

MAR

By Nancy Cato and published by New English Library

All the Rivers Run
Forefathers
North-West by South
Brown Sugar
A Distant Island
The Heart of the Continent

NANCY CATO
MARIGOLD

NEW ENGLISH LIBRARY

British Library Cataloguing in Publication Data

Cato, Nancy
  Marigold.
  I. Title
  823 [F]

  ISBN 0-450-56407-X

Published by New English Library,
a hardcover imprint of Hodder and Stoughton,
a division of Hodder and Stoughton Ltd,
Mill Road, Dunton Green, Sevenoaks, Kent TN13 2YA.
Editorial Office: 47 Bedford Square, London WC1B 3DP.

Photoset by Rowland Phototypesetting Ltd,
Bury St Edmunds, Suffolk.

Printed in Great Britain by
BPCC Hazells Ltd, Member of BPCC Ltd

Author's Note

This story is set in a city which no longer exists. It is a period piece from before the days of refrigerators or the Pill. It could be called the Age of Innocence. Before drugs, before schoolgirl sex, before Adelaide had an Arts Festival; when overseas travel was by ship only, except for a few hardy adventurers who went by flying-boat to London.

The city was more like a large, prosperous country town set on the edge of a vast wheat farm. Vineyards and olive and almond groves grew in the suburbs, on the gentle slopes of the foothills, and wineries flourished though not many people drank table wines. Port, sherry and beer were more popular and most of the wine was exported.

Anyway you were not permitted to drink alcohol after 6 p.m., or 7 p.m. with a meal. Serious wine-drinkers bought the local claret and hock, which were good, or imported their drink from France. And if you tried to eat out after 7.30 at night the choice in the city was restricted to a pie-cart or a sandwich bar.

All this has changed, changed utterly. Adelaide has any number of excellent restaurants, and coffee, since the Italians came, tastes like coffee and not like dishwater. Good wine has replaced sherry as a popular drink. *Ulysses* is no longer banned; poets read their works in the parklands. Adelaide has come of age.

And that is journalism . . . it comes to selling your soul, your intellect, and your opinions.

Balzac, *Lost Illusions*

One

We must have been an unlucky family, starting with the ancestor who fell over his claymore at the Battle of Culloden and did himself an unfortunate injury, he wearing only a kilt at the time.

When they buried my youngest uncle they could have saved money by using a child's coffin, for though he was a grown man he had been bitten in half by a shark; only his top half was recovered. However he was interred decently in a full-sized coffin. I know because I was taken to the funeral at the age of about four.

I watched with detached interest the shiny box being lowered into the deep hole, thinking what a waste to put all that gleaming silver and polished wood in the ground where no one would see it. My mother and Aunt Flora were crying into their handkerchiefs. Death was a mysterious and unreal concept to me; I just knew I didn't like the look of that gaping hole. Flowers had been strewn on the coffin lid, and my mother handed me an arum lily to throw after them. Then my second uncle, with misplaced zeal, picked me up and held me over the grave so that I could more easily drop my floral tribute.

1

Still clutching the lily, I began to scream with terror. I was afraid he would drop me into the grave; I was carried away, sobbing, by my tall father in his comforting arms. I adored my father, who was often away up north, visiting properties in the far corners of the State. I used to kiss his photograph every night until he returned.

I knew what had happened to my uncle because I'd heard them discuss it, and my father saying, "You know, if that shark had been hungrier we'd never have known what happened to Fred."

Next came the death of my father while I was still a schoolgirl. I knew little about it except that he had been killed in an accident. I supposed they meant an accident with a car. I was sent off to Aunt Flora for a few days, until the funeral was over; I was relieved about this, as from my one experience I did not think much of these rites of occasions. At the time we were living uneventfully in the suburbs – myself, the spoilt and only child, my mother, and my father, who was older than Mother and already grey-haired. Then there was Ruby who was the maid but regarded herself as one of the family, only better. I believe she stayed with us out of kindness, and because she was fond of Mother while regarding her as a hopeless incompetent. Probably she couldn't bear to think of the mess the place would get into if she were to leave. So she stayed on, sweeping up broken china and the "artistic" arrangements of flowers that my mother would keep setting in precarious positions on window-sills or narrow shelves.

Every Tuesday Aunt Flora came to visit and stayed all day. She was about as wide as she was high and short of breath, with a high-coloured complexion and a voice to match.

She would arrive in mid-morning, having caught an early tram from her home on the other side of Adelaide. She was always laden with paper bags bursting with yeast buns, cream cakes and something called "iced logs",

2

bought in town when she changed trams. She seemed convinced that there were no cakes to be had in our house, though in fact Mother was a good cook and baked once a week. Her butterfly-cakes, light enough to fly away, with two dainty wings of sponge-cake embedded in fresh cream – I can taste them still. I liked them far better than Aunt Flora's offerings: solid cakes of an unlikely deep yellow with bright pink icing, or puffs filled with highly synthetic cream.

I used to think that Mother ate cream buns as a sort of compensation for the blows life had dealt her – losing her favourite brother and then her husband; and her great sorrow, that she never had a son. I would have given anything to be a boy, but I had turned out wrong and there was nothing to be done about it.

Aunt Flora's addiction was harder to explain, as she was always sighing about her weight and her "poor legs" which had to carry it. Even when her brother died she must have rather enjoyed the sensation it caused, for she loved to be the bearer of ill tidings: "Archie's girl – you remember Archie? – has a growth, they'll have to remove *everything*!" she would announce dramatically. I could imagine her going round the relatives when Uncle Fred died: "I always said he was asking for trouble, he *would* go out too far, and now look what's happened."

My father didn't like Aunt Flora – they didn't get on, Mother said vaguely – so she was usually gone before he returned from his office in the city.

Meanwhile I had begun to grow rapidly – outgrowing her strength it was called. From a chubby four-year-old I became a skinny seven, with bony arms and legs and a pale face powdered with freckles. My only good point was my red hair, which was naturally curly. I was quite healthy, but Mother decided that I was "a delicate child" and subjected me to a series of nauseous cure-alls.

One drug which she hoped would make a big strong girl of me was Thyroid Extract. It came in the form of hard grey tablets, which she hopefully crushed in a teaspoon of strawberry jam. As they had a particularly strong and unpleasant smell, the only result was to put me off strawberry jam for life. Like the aperient wrapped in silver paper to look like chocolate, which I trustingly took into my infant mouth, it simply tasted like medicine.

But my mother was a determined woman, and she kept up the thyroid treatment for a month. The tablets were probably some quack remedy with little more in them than calcium; but at this stage of my development, no doubt due to natural growth, my hands suddenly became bigger, too large for my thin little wrists, and my ears also increased in size. Mother, anxiously re-reading the label, found that the thyroid extract was supposed to come from the glands of monkeys.

Immediately deciding that her child was developing simian features, to my relief she stopped the treatment and buried the rest of the pills in the garden. She had given up trying to make me take cod liver oil and Clements' Tonic but tried every new health food on me – things like Bemax and Robolene, with a taste not so much revolting as peculiar – and finally a dried milk and vitamin concoction which looked exactly like mouse-droppings. After a while I managed to knock over the tin where it was kept on a shelf in a kitchen cupboard. Most of it spilled down to the bottom of the cupboard, and when Ruby was spring-cleaning she swept it all up and set a mouse trap there.

I still remained obstinately thin and pale, so my mother gave up and pinned her faith on plenty of milk (which I loathed), and porridge with butter and cream.

When my father died I was nine years old and going to a girls' school not far from my home on the first slopes of the foothills. I walked to school across several empty paddocks, for the city was only just beginning to spread this far. I was kept away from school for more than a week. At last I had to go back and face the half-shamed sympathy of those whose fathers were still alive. My best

4

friend Dinah blushed to the roots of her yellow plaits as she muttered some gruff words. We both felt it wasn't done to lose a close member of your family. It was quite embarrassing, in fact.

My father's death did not seem real to me. He was often away in the country, and I was inured to his absences. Now I expected to come back and find everything the same as before. But of course it wasn't.

Ruby was openly discontented, saying she missed having a man about the place, and Mother's eyes were often red. I missed him too, but it was more like a toothache that goes on and on until you gradually get used to it. And everything had not been perfect in our home before. I was aware of the tensions in the grown-up world without ever understanding them. I remembered the time the double bed was taken out of the front room and the two single beds took its place. Not long after this my father moved into a room of his own.

It seemed to me a happy arrangement, for I was given to nightmares and would run into Mother's bed for comfort. The next night my father shouted something angrily from the bedroom door, and Mother sat down on her rose-pink bedspread and wept bitterly.

"Why did Daddy make you cry?" I kept asking, but she wouldn't answer.

About two years after my father's death Mother told me "that nice Mr Hackett who always brings us chocolates" would be moving in as my new Daddy. I didn't mind (though I couldn't see the necessity of having him sleep in the house) for besides chocolates he used sometimes to bring me a book, once a big fat *Schoolgirl's Own Annual* with enough reading in it for a week. The present of a book was a sure path to my heart.

Mere printed words fascinated me. If I couldn't find anything else I would read the newspapers, right down to the fine print and the advertisements. I even read an old volume of Ouida, with art nouveau binding and Gothic illustrations, which I found down the cellar. It was quite a short book and I wolfed it in an hour, skipping over any words or phrases I didn't understand (such as *et tu Brute!* which I translated to my own satisfaction as "Oh, thou brute!").

My stepfather-to-be was in Insurance, and was full of statistics of life expectancy, accident potential, and the incidence of fire, flood and earthquake. I believe worrying about these things had made him rather dried-up and dyspeptic. He was nothing like my big, jolly father.

Mr Hackett told Mother that the chances of being bitten in half by a shark were almost nil, less than those of being fatally bitten by a snake. I think he thought the uniqueness of his end might comfort her over the death of Uncle Fred.

After the wedding I was packed off to Aunt Flora's while they went away without me. They always seemed to want to get me out of the way.

I hated staying with Aunt Flora, who was long widowed and was terribly fussy about wiping your feet before coming inside, and polishing the glasses till they sparkled when washing up. She had a horrid little yappy Pomeranian dog, which would lie under the table and growl at me all through every meal. I was sure it was just getting up courage to take my ankle in its teeth.

Getting up for a drink of water on my first night there (for I didn't dare call out for one as I would have at home), I heard Aunt Flora talking on her bedside telephone: "Yes, I've got her here again for a week or two. I had her the other time, till that business blew over . . . It doesn't seem long, does it . . . No . . . Still, I suppose they waited two years . . . No, she doesn't know a thing about it. Let's hope she never knows the whole story, poor child."

My ears felt stretched and enormous as I waited in the dark hall. Though I didn't understand, the "poor child" was me. I listened for more, but Aunt Flora went on to talk about her favourite subject, food. I crept back to bed.

The room had a high window, and sitting up and nursing my cold feet, I saw for the first time in my life the nearly full moon high in the east. I was usually in bed at this time and my room was shaded by a verandah. I had no idea the moon could be so brilliant, so enormous, so silver-white. I stared at it, puzzling over my aunt's strange words. What had been kept from me?

Soft wisps of cloud drifted across the face of the moon without dimming its glory.

"O moon!" I said, addressing it in the vocative case. I stared upward in a trance of worship, my aunt's words receding.

> "O moon! What tongue can praise thee?
> The clouds kneel before thee
> All things adore thee,
> Heaven and earth are full of thy glory
> And thy glorious light."

After this pagan chant I must have fallen asleep still sitting up, for I woke some time later, cold, with my head at the wrong end of the bed, and the moon gone from the window.

I remembered vaguely Aunt Flora's phone conversation but it would be useless to ask questions. "Little pitchers have big ears," she would say, or "Least said soonest mended," one of those maddening meaningless sayings with which her speech was sprinkled. Such as "Children should be seen and not heard," only in this case I had heard and not been seen.

On my first night home again I lay on the floor of the kitchen, where Ruby was sitting at the table working at pen-painting – making fiddly pink and white roses with oil paint, applying them with a pen nib to black cloth doyleys. They were for her "glory-box" which she kept in her room, full of things like embroidered pillow-slips and tablecloths for when she got married. It seemed that old people, as I thought of them, all got married eventually.

I didn't see why you needed painted doyleys, though. I read what was left of the morning paper – for the front pages had disappeared – and had reached the small advertisements at the back, when at the end of a Birth Notice I came on a strange new word.

"What's 'stillborn' mean, Ruby?" I asked idly.

To my surprise she giggled and ducked her head over her work. "Never you mind," she said.

"But why? What's it mean?"

"You ask your Ma in nine months' time and she may be able to tell you; but let's hope not," she added mysteriously.

"Why nine months?" I asked. "She'll tell me straight away."

In the morning I went to Mother's room as usual, and climbed into her bed to dip a biscuit in her cup of morning tea. To my surprise the double bed had come back, and the new Daddy was sleeping in it.

I wriggled down into the crook of Mother's arm, meaning to ask her what that word meant and why Ruby was so silly. The new Daddy lifted his head from the pillow a moment, said "Hello, youngster," then heaved over the other way with his back to us.

"Tell me what you did at Aunty Flora's. Did you help her in the garden?" asked Mother.

"Yes, I watered the lawn." (And I had hosed that stupid little dog, though I didn't tell her that.)

I felt the bed to be unbearably hot with three people in it. It was stifling under the blankets, I couldn't breathe. I felt myself getting hot, hotter, hotter until in a moment I would burst into flames.

I struggled out of the bed and ran back to my own room.

"What's the matter, dear?" I heard behind me, but I couldn't explain. I never visited Mother in the early morn-

8

ing again, and the question about "stillborn" was never asked.

Some months later Mother told me in a brief, embarrassed way that I could expect a little sister or brother before too long. She hoped it would be a brother. By this time my sex education had been taken in hand by some slightly older girls at school, and though some of the details were a bit inaccurate – I was solemnly informed that the usual position for couples was back to back – I got the general idea.

From then on I never asked questions of anyone older when I came across strange words like "rape" and "abortion". With the help of a dictionary I worked things out for myself.

When Celia arrived she was not so bad as babies go, but she grew into an obnoxious brat with black curls and a milk-and-roses complexion.

This alone was enough to make me dislike her, since I have red hair and a face as pale as curds. Besides, Celia had the unfair advantage of being born with these big innocent blue eyes, so that she could tell a whopping lie and everyone believed her.

The gap in years was too big for us to be friends. The year when I turned seventeen, and began in what promised to be the glamorous and exciting career of a cadet reporter, Celia was still only six – a mere infant.

All that reading of newspapers now gave me an advantage. I felt I would take to journalism like a duck to water.

Two

Some time after my seventeenth birthday I started as a "cub", or cadet, the lowest form of literary life in the newspaper world, on an evening paper called the *Standard*. Not thinking of its other meaning as a flag or a banner, I decided that this name meant the newspaper had high standards, "style recognised as the criterion of what is best, in speech, action, taste etc."

I had made up my mind that instead of a stage career or that of an explorer (two possibilities I had toyed with) I wanted to Write. And experience as a junior reporter would give me plenty of training.

I bought a new fountain pen and resolved to save up my pay for a second-hand portable typewriter. The office provided typewriters for its literary staff, large cumbersome machines of great antiquity. I had a fairly good one, but sometimes after I'd been out on an assignment I would find the Chaffcutter sitting on my desk. This was an ancient wheezing contraption which jumped letters and stuck halfway through words. I would go rampaging round the office till I found the culprit who had "borrowed" mine – usually one of the Phone Room boys, who sat all day, earphones in place, taking down phoned-in reports direct on to the typewriter.

I couldn't touch-type as yet, and preferred using my fountain pen though the ink was inclined to soak into the copy-paper provided. Mostly I found myself taking notes with the shiny lead pencils provided by the Chief of Staff. He had an endless supply in a drawer in his desk.

On my very first assignment I turned in five paragraphs of polished prose on an event which had already been covered by our rival. I'd scarcely reached the door of the Subs' Room after dropping my story proudly in the wire basket when Mr Ryan called me back.

"Miss *Trent*! Do you really think this item's worth all these breathless paragraphs? Most of it has been in the *Recorder* already, you know. Try to remember this is a newspaper, not a women's magazine."

I edged out, feeling crushed, and paused outside the door to recover my composure. Then I heard the same Sub say in quite a mild voice, "You have to put the fear of God into these cubs."

Now I was learning to "keep it brief" as we were always being urged to do.

"Chief wants to see you, Miss Trent."

I picked up a wad of copy-paper and a chewed pencil and made my way to the glass-enclosed sanctum of the Chief of Staff. How often had he already sent for me? I had only just arrived, having merely glanced at the front page of the *Recorder*, the morning paper, while bolting my breakfast.

The Chief was busy giving an assignment to someone else, so I stood in front of his desk and tried to read upside down several items with circles drawn round them in the *Recorder*, which was spread in front of him.

Then one of the phones on the desk rang. Mr Parfitt

answered it, looking vaguely up at me under his brows as he murmured, "Yes, yairs . . . that's right. Yairs."

There was nothing more exciting to look forward to than a ring to the Prince George Hospital for accident cases, and a visit to the Public Library, Museum and Art Gallery, which with the Zoo were lumped together on my round.

Where was the excitement, the glamour I had expected? All my reading so far had led me to believe that journalists spent their lives solving murder mysteries single-handed.

Now I leant a hip against the Chief's table, feeling much older and wiser than when I'd started work a month ago, and a lot less starry-eyed.

The Chief himself looked nothing like a Hollywood eye-shaded city-desk type. He had black curly hair and a bumpy forehead, a slow voice and a vague manner. His teeth were small and even, with a space between the front ones like a child's.

"Ah, Marigold!" said Mr Parfitt at last, slowly putting the receiver back on the stand. He ruffled his dark curls with one hand as if to stir some ideas under his scalp. "Er – I suppose you saw this par in the *Recorder* this morning about the chimps at the Zoo having a domestic tiff?"

I made a noncommittal noise. I hadn't seen a thing. The Chief groped for a cigarette smouldering in his ashtray, his eyes still on the paper spread before him. "Should be a follow-up there. Pictures too; you'd better take John Dickson with you. See if Sarah's off her food, what damage she did to her old man – light stuff, with plenty of colour and human interest."

I said coldly, "*Human* interest, Mr Parfitt?"

"Eh? Yes, you know the sort of thing. And meet the Overland express and ring the hotels for Personals. And if there's not much doing on your round you can help the Social Editress this afternoon. Better look in at the WCTU meeting first. This morning there's a meeting of the Boy Scouts Association being opened by the Governor. You'd better cover that. His Ex. never says anything important, but you never know.

"Oh, and Marigold!" he called me back as I was going out. "Keep it brief, will you? Space is tight as hell."

Boy Scouts! The Zoo! The love-life of the chimpanzee! How could I write deathless prose about such subjects? I went off, muttering under my breath.

I searched for the item about the mis-mated chimpanzees, cut it out of my paper with a razor-blade, stuffed some copy-paper and a pencil in my handbag, and collected the photographer from Pictorial.

He didn't like the Zoo either; but when we got there the artist in him was aroused, and he insisted on taking the flamingos reflected in their pool, as well as the chimpanzees.

Sam, the wife-beating chimp, refused to come out into the light at first, sulking in the back of his cage; and with this and waiting for the reflections it was after eleven when we got back to the office.

I banged out the Zoo story on my typewriter, then hurried to the Boy Scouts Association meeting. Going up the steps of the hall I met the representative of the *Recorder* coming down. In theory he was a deadly rival.

"Ah, I hoped it would be you, Marigold," said the large, untidy, saintly-looking person with silver hair known as "The Bish". ("Because of my alleged episcopal appearance," he would explain, "and the numbers of Church conferences I have covered.") "Fact is, I couldn't stay for the Governor's speech, I've got an article to finish for an early page. Dear girl, be a sport and cover it for me, will you? He won't say anything startling – never does."

"All right, Bish. But you'll be found out one day."

He twinkled at me through his silver-rimmed glasses, and trotted off down the steps in an odour of whisky.

I was late for the meeting but I didn't care. I entered as unobtrusively as possible from the back of the hall, but an officious khaki-clad male who knew me by sight hurried up and led me to the Press table in front. The Governor, who was in the middle of a well-polished peroration, frowned slightly. First one Press representative left before his speech was half begun; now another arrived when it was nearly over.

"Ah-hem," he said significantly. "The – er – undoubted benefit to the boys of the community, who will be the – ah – soldiers of the future."

He smoothed back his heavy military moustache with a final gesture. When he had sat down amid a round of applause, I tiptoed to the end of the row where the Governor's secretary sat, and asked him for the text of the speech, since I had missed the beginning.

Mr Nelson was not an obliging man; he disliked reporters, but realised they were necessary evils. "All right; I'll see," he muttered ungraciously.

I went through the Treasurer's report on the table, trying once more to make out what made a balance-sheet balance; it always looked like cheating to me, the way the figures added up exactly.

During the round of clapping after the annual report was read, Mr Nelson approached the Governor at the edge of the low platform. Watching, I saw his red face turn a shade redder, while he whispered a violent remark.

The secretary came back and murmured in my ear, "He won't give it to you."

"Why not? What did he say?"

"He said . . ." Mr Nelson looked like a malicious cherub with his round pink cheeks and sharp blue eyes. "He said, 'Tell that red-headed girl to get here on time in future.'"

"Oh! And you tell *him* that my hair isn't this colour for nothing. He'll see!"

And gathering up my papers I marched out.

On the way back to the office I planned revenge. When the story was written, and dropped like a time-bomb in the Chief Sub's basket, I went back to find a note on my table:

The Editress of the Women's Magazine will not be lunching out today, but intends consuming a pie in her room.

I had already sent out for a cheese and gherkin roll and an apple slice, but was not surprised, on looking into the package delivered by an aloof copy-boy, to find a beef roll and a repulsive-looking cream cake.

I went down the corridor again and through the composing room where the linotype-machines were clicking and tapping busily, unerringly picking up the letters with their long metal arms. They looked like other-world monsters in the eerie blue light of the neon tubes.

Along a second corridor I came to an inside room where an electric light, with an ugly white reflector, burned perpetually. Darkness at noon . . . Roma was reclined at ease in her swivel-chair, eating a pie.

"'Day, Mal. Take a seat."

My friends had always called me "Mal" at school, finding my real name far too long and difficult; to me it just sounded friendly. For the same reason, or lack of reason, I usually called Roma "Stan" rather than her rather classic-sounding Christian name.

"Thanks, Stan," I said gloomily, gazing into my paper bag.

"Had a good day, old thing?"

"Rotten! The Zoo again."

"*Mein Gott!* The elephant has croup, I suppose . . . No, don't tell me! The Princess Alexandra parrot is *enceinte* once more."

"No. Chimpanzees."

I resisted an urge to tell Roma what I had just done; she would only try to persuade me to go and get my copy back before it was too late. I sighed and frowned and put my feet up among a cluster of damp galley-proofs on the corner of her desk.

"I have to help old Myfanwy this afternoon. And before that, the Women's Temperance Union's annual meeting."

"Well, cheer up."

"No, but honestly, Stan! The stuff they waste the space on, and they keep moaning that space is tight! Comic strips and bathing beauties, horseracing and football, social notes and animal stories! God, I wish I could get sent to the courts to cover murders, or something."

"Heaven forbid!"

"Well, at least death is real."

"Never mind. Perhaps the chimpanzees will die of their croup."

I dropped the front two legs of my chair to the floor with a bang. "If they don't give me a good story to cover soon, I – I'll make one! You'll see. I'll rob the Art Gallery, or something."

"Yes, Mal, but if you don't mind I've got to make up a couple of pages in half an hour –"

"Oh, don't let me keep you from your important work."

Slightly offended, I dropped the paper bag with the remains of my lunch into her wastepaper basket, and departed. Anyway, it was nearly time for the WCTU meeting.

At Grapejuice Hall the Little White Ribboners were singing, a band of prim small girls with white bows in their hair:

> O fight the Demon Drink
> Until he falls!
> Let not the Demon Drink
> Within your walls . . .

Across the back of the hall was a banner with large red lettering, BEER IS BEST, and in small letters underneath, LEFT ALONE.

The theme of the president's address was the wickedness of *vignerons* who turned nourishing fruit into a social poison. She was a thin, plain woman with rather a red and shiny nose. She poured some grape juice into a glass and drank it with exaggerated pleasure, then washed it down with water. Every true housewife and mother, she said, would refuse to have fermented liquor in the house.

I took a few notes, but I knew the speech would receive scant space in either the *Standard* or the morning paper. Most journalists like a drink, and a Wine Week rates more space than a Temperance Rally, if only because of the winegrowers' advertisements. And Adelaide was surrounded by vineyards.

Sometimes I wondered about the things that found a space on Page One. A kitten trapped in a stormwater drain, a puppy rescued from a well, rated a 28-point head and a picture; while tucked away on an inside page, a laconic three lines would record that a million people had perished in a year of famine in India.

Animal stories plus "human interest", and a bit of pathos or whimsicality were sure to be featured.

"You must remember," Mr Smythe the Assistant Editor had told me on my first day, "that you are writing for a readership with an average age of fourteen years – and that's being over-generous to the mental age of most of our readers. They don't want to think; they want to be amused. Human interest, with a good murder now and then and a few suicides for general interest – that's what sells an evening paper."

"But don't you think," I objected, "that details of murder trials tend to make unbalanced people go and do likewise? And I do think reports of suicides, with dotted lines where the body fell, are rather hard on the relatives."

"They are the things that sell papers, and circulation is what counts," said Mr Smythe imperturbably.

It was then that I began to think there was something rather hard about his mouth under its neat grey moustache, and a coldness about his pale grey eyes – steely was the word.

17

"Still keen on your job?" he would bark at me when we met in the corridor. "That's the girl. A journalist must always be keen."

This had been the burden of his cry when I had my first interview for the cadetship; also that of "We're just one big, happy family here."

"Keenness, accuracy, speed," Mr Smythe had intoned. "And the greatest of these is keenness. Now here's the *Standard*'s style sheet. Keep it as a guide."

I took the printed sheet from him. "We do *not* use," I read, "the phrases:

a sickening thud
a shot rang out
an agonised scream
a hardened criminal
a breathless chase
as white as snow
as black as ink . . ."

"We don't use them because they're journalistic clichés," Mr Smythe explained. "We avoid them like the plague. I used to keep on telling every new cadet about them, but they still turned up with monotonous regularity. At last I gave up the unequal struggle and had the style sheet printed."

I had put it in my bag, thinking that I'd heard rather often some of the phrases just used by the Assistant Editor. Still the style sheet showed that the paper had literary standards; no doubt most of the Subs wrote little master-pieces in their spare time.

"You will be treated as a man," Mr Smythe had assured me. "You must expect no special privileges, as you will be paid exactly the same as the men on the staff."

This pleased me very much, as I had always wanted to be a boy. But I soon found that a policy of segregation was kept up.

Instead of a desk in the Reporters' Room, I was given

a corner of a table in the Social Room. There I was in the rather daunting presence of Myfanwy Jones, the Social Editress, who knew the family tree of every person of importance in our small city, and was on first-name terms with most of them.

And here I was at the Women's Christian Temperance Union, and not a man in sight.

I was impatient to get back to the office and see the first edition the moment it came off the press. As soon as the hour of the "death-knock" had passed – that is, the time after which the last edition would irrevocably have gone to press – I made my escape. Even if the roof had fallen in on the Temperance meeting it would be of no use for the *Standard*; Today's News Today was the paper's slogan.

At the office I grabbed a copy of the first edition, smelling magically of still-wet ink, and made for the women's room. There, locked safely in the lavatory, I unfolded the paper. I looked briefly and disgustedly at the chimpanzee item, featured with a picture on the front page, and then turned to the Edition page.

There it was! The large three-column headline said:

SIR GEORGE MARTINET GIVES £100
TO BOY SCOUTS
Governor's Generous Patronage

Triumphantly I read it through. Now the Bish had only to copy it for tomorrow's *Recorder*, and everyone would believe it. The Governor could hardly deny it without looking mean and foolish.

I lurked in the lavatory for a while, but decided that if there was going to be a row I might as well come out and face it. To give me strength I bought a couple of chocolate frogs from Freddie Flannigan, who kept a store of them under his counter for sale to hungry members of the staff. He ruled with an iron hand the row of copy-boys who sat on the bench in the Dogbox awaiting errands. He was known as Freddo, not only because he sold frogs but because with his squat figure and rather bulging eyes, he resembled one.

I went back to the Social Room and wrote blocklines for pictures of beaming Saturday brides.

"It's a blessing you could help me today, dear, as Helen's not here," said Myfanwy, puffing at the cigarette in its long holder.

Every moment I expected a boy to arrive beside my table with the message: "Miss Trent, the Editor wishes to see you at once."

But the afternoon passed away peacefully in a maze of Social Notes. The Late edition was printing, and the building shook with a faint trembling roar. The giant rolls of paper were whizzing round, and in a blur of white and grey recorded a hundred thousand times that Mrs Arthur Pratt had left for a holiday in the East, that disarmament talks had failed once more, that the Governor had given £100 to the Boy Scouts Association . . . Soon everyone would be reading the paper, even the inhabitants of Government House.

I could just imagine Lady Martinet giving H.E. a piece of her mind: "A hundred pounds to the Boy Scouts, and I can't even have a new outfit for the Cup! I could understand it if it were the Girl Guides Association, they have a very attractive Commissioner this year . . ."

Three

Next day I was up at dawn, waiting for the *Recorder* to be delivered. I snatched it away from the dog (who wanted to have a game) and unrolled it with a trembling hand. What if there was a denial?

Good old Bish! There was my story, in slightly different terms, beginning:

SURPRISE BEQUEST BY GOVERNOR
Boy Scouts Benefit

Surprise, all right! I knew who was surprised.

I arrived at the office so early that Howard Miller affected to fall beneath the newspaper-files in a fit.

"Ye Gods! She is early! How did you do it, child? Did you stay up all night, or what?"

"Ass! I got up early to read the paper, as every good reporter should. Keenness, accuracy, speed. And the greatest of these – "

"Yes! Mr Smythe."

The Chief complimented me on scooping the *Recorder*, and suggested a follow-up.

"Wonder the *Recorder* didn't hop on to it. Ring up the

Boy Scouts Association and see what they propose doing with the donation, will you?"

"I certainly will," I said. "With pleasure."

"Anything on the train? You got Brewster the violinist, did you?"

"Yes. He had some hard things to say about our Railways. He was in one of the old carriages."

"Good. Ring the Hospital about that old chap who was knocked down by a bus last night, condition critical. If he's going to die, he might do it in the *Standard's* time . . . Now, er –" He turned over a page and groped for the item through a fog of cigarette smoke coming from the butt between his lips. "Ah! Here – this bit about the swarms of flying-ants in the city last night. Should be a follow-up there. Light scientific stuff, you know. See that chap at the Museum, the – er, etymologist or something."

"The entomologist," I said, for I could never resist showing off superior knowledge.

"Eh? Yes, chap who specialises in insects. Anything doing on your round?"

"Not unless someone robbed the Art Gallery or murdered the Museum Director. You know nothing ever happens on my round."

"That's not true," he said seriously. "There was that fight between the chimps at the Zoo yesterday. Good story."

"Is that *all*, Mr Parfitt?" I asked bitterly.

At the Museum I made my way to the entomologist's room along a dark downstairs corridor where bones and skeletons lay on shelves, and painted casts of Aborigines' torsos stared at me through the gloom.

I found Mr McAirdle admiring a huge model in wax of a revolting-looking green bug he told me was a Lucerne Flea. Asked about the swarms of flying-ants dancing about the street lights and falling in heaps to the ground, he waxed technical in a broad Scots accent on the mating habits of flying-ants:

22

"Then the female bites off her ain wings, ye ken, and crawls into a wee crrack to lay her aigs and stairt the new colony."

"But that's horrible!" I cried.

"Eh? Whyfor is it horrible? It's Nature, my gel."

"Then I don't think much of Nature. Fancy being able to fly, and then *biting off your own wings* on purpose!"

"It's for the new generation, ye see. Nature is only concairned with the species, not the indiveedual."

On the way back to the office I called at the Art Gallery, where I skipped down the marble inside stairs to the office of the Director. He was a large, vigorous, cheerful man with bright expressive eyes and a lively mind, who always managed to cheer me up. I concluded that he must be very old, for he was quite bald but for a few wisps of grey about the edges of his shiny scalp.

"Hullo, any news?" I asked. "Bought any Botticellis lately?"

"This girl is always pestering the life out of me for news," grumbled Mr Muecke to his secretary. "I tell her that Rembrandt painted a great picture called *The Night Watch*, and she says it isn't news."

"It might have been, three hundred years ago," I said, and intoned after Mr Smythe: "News is anything new, strange, or interesting. If a dog bites a man, that is not news; but if a man bites a dog – "

"I'm damned if I'm going to bite a dog just so you can get a story out of me for your paper," said Mr Muecke.

I laughed. "Come on now, you must have something. Strange, interesting, or new?"

"Well, there's a rather nice T'ang horse been donated to the ceramics section. Like to see it?"

He led me upstairs and through a forest of glass cases filled with china and glass, porcelain and jade. He stopped beside a locked case and inserted a key.

"There it is," he said, holding up the statuette. "A little beauty, and perfectly preserved. See what a spirited arch to the neck and back – full of life, after hundreds of years."

I touched the terracotta horse reverently. It was the spirit of all horses, in the fragile form of baked clay. I noted down the name of the donor and a few more facts.

Mr Muecke looked at me thoughtfully as he put the figure back in the case.

"I've been wondering," he said, "whether I used to know your Dad. Wasn't he interested in art – collected some aboriginal paintings from Hermannsburg before they were fashionable?"

"That's right. He had one or two early Prentices too. He was manager of Bailey and Disher, the stock and station people."

"Of course! Harvey Trent – I met him up at Alice Springs, years ago. His hair was the same colour as yours."

"Oh no! His hair was grey."

"It was red – sorry, auburn – when I knew him first."

"He died when I was quite young, but I only remember it as grey."

"Yes, it was a sad business when he –" Mr Muecke stopped and made a great business of locking up the case. "That's rather valuable, you know, can't have it getting stolen. Even if it *would* make a good story for your paper. Come downstairs and I'll lend you a print to go with the T'ang horse item."

I was intrigued by the thought of my tall father with his bristly moustache that used to tickle me when he kissed me goodnight, having once been young, with hair as carroty as my own. Sometimes, these days, I almost forgot my "step" was not my real father. He was just as possessive and interfering as if I had been his own daughter, and an absolute despot in the home.

I wrote the T'ang horse story for an early page for the following day, something that could be set in type straight away to fill some of the blank spaces the ad-men were already ruling up on their little model pages.

I dropped it rather diffidently in the Subs' basket. Art did not rate as high as lost kittens or disaffected chimpanzees, and nowhere near as high as footballers or the birth of a son to a leading jockey's wife.

On the way out I passed a sheaf of damp galley proofs hanging from a spring-clip by the door. A heading ran lengthwise down one of them: VIOLINIST HITS AT OUR TRAINS. It was my interview with the visiting maestro. I closed my eyes on a vision of the little man swiping at a passing train with his fiddle-bow.

I'd sent a boy out for some lunch, so while ringing the Public Hospital to check again on the bus victim, I peeled a banana and took a large bite. Just then the Switchboard answered. I asked in a muffled voice for Casualty. At that moment the Editor himself came in the door of the Social Room.

This august being rarely spoke to cub reporters. He was a big man with a slow smile and blue eyes which also smiled. His voice was deep and authoritative, and I held him in great awe. While everyone on the staff smoked while working, eating was somehow shameful, I felt.

With a tremendous effort I pushed the whole of the banana into my mouth and swallowed. I looked up at the Editor with an expression of bright inquiry. (My mouth was too full for smiling.) At that moment Casualty answered.

"Gugnorning ither Sthandard offush here,' I mumbled.

"Hullo? Casualty! Hullo?"

"Ither –" But a piece of banana went down the wrong way, I coughed violently, and the piece sailed out of my mouth and made a graceful landing on the telephone.

I looked up agitatedly, my face going scarlet.

"Nemmind, I'll callgen laterer," I gasped, and hung up.

Mr Perceval's mouth was clamped on his pipe, but an amused twinkle lurked in his blue eyes. "Hullo, Marigold. Busy?"

"Er – no, I mean yes! I have to be at a meeting in five minutes. I was just –"

"Well, come in and see me when you get back, will you? Don't worry, it's nothing disastrous," he said as my eyes widened in alarm. He took out the pipe, waved it reassuringly, and ambled out.

"I'll have dreadful indigestion after this!" said my stepfather, glaring at the dinner on his plate.

"Well, you don't have to eat it, dear. There's some nice barley broth in the kitchen, I'll just heat it up –"

"No, no, a man has to put something solid in his stomach, I suppose," he said, taking a mouthful of braised steak with the air of a martyr.

"I still don't see," he added, turning to me, "why you didn't take on this new women's magazine page if it meant a higher salary."

"Money isn't everything," I muttered. We had been over this before, as soon as I'd been foolish enough to boast about the "promotion" Mr Perceval had offered me.

"No doubt," said my stepfather drily. "But it serves to buy the food you are eating."

I stopped eating at once. It was true I did not pay any board at home, so that I was able to save money.

"I hate women's page stuff, fashions and recipes and what people wore at the races –"

"I always find the Social pages interesting," said Mother mildly. "Much nicer than all these strikes and murders and accidents and things."

"I wish they'd give me something more exciting to do," I said. "Now if I were a police roundsman –"

"Heaven forbid!" said Mother.

My stepfather looked at me through his bifocals, tilting his head back for better focus. This made him look arrogant, though it was only caused by being half-blind.

"What an idea! Why, all sorts of unsavoury cases come up, and a young girl like you should not –"

"Good heavens, Dad, I'm not a child!"

26

"You're not grown up, so there!" said Celia instantly.

"I am grown up, Miss Impertinence."

"She's not. No one is legally grown up till they're twenty-one, are they, Daddy?"

"Legally, no. Legally Marigold's a minor, and her life expectancy is excellent, barring accidents."

"I'm old enough to earn my own living, and to have a driving licence."

He always managed to make me feel rebellious, with his fierce eyebrows and dictatorial manner. Mother and Celia seemed not to mind his mild bullying. They obeyed his loud pronouncements at the time, and quietly went their own way later.

"That's another thing," he said. "This mad idea of spending all your money on some rattletrap of a second-hand car. It's simply a waste. But fools and their money are soon parted."

"It isn't a waste. I need a car in my work, and the office pays a good mileage allowance. And Sandy Martin is teaching me to drive."

"*That* young scatterbrain! These young fools shouldn't be allowed on the public road. A menace to themselves and everyone else."

"Sandy's never had an accident."

While we argued, Mother had quietly removed the plates to the service hatch and fetched the cherry pie, with a golden crinkled crust and a dusting of sparkling sugar. I couldn't make a pie like that to save my life, and never thought of learning.

Food was unimportant, I considered, never having known the want of it. I couldn't stand the long boring conversations Mother and Aunt Flora had on the telephone about it, and I hated to be called in from watching a sunset for such a mundane purpose as eating. My head was stuffed with poetry and all I wanted was food for the soul. Nevertheless I made a good dinner.

"And another thing, young lady," said my stepfather,

taking a large helping of cream with his pie, "you needn't
expect me to pay your repair bills, and there'll be plenty
of them. And I don't want you spending all your time on
this car, and never helping your mother in the house."
(For Ruby had got married, departed, and never been
replaced.)

"Why can't Celia help? She's not working all day like I
am."

Celia poked out her tongue at me, then used it to lick
cherry juice from her spoon. "Look at her!" I said disgustedly, noting the healthy pink of her tongue and her
aggressively rosy cheeks. (Her father was convinced that
my natural pallor was caused by late nights, and would
remark irritatingly, "Celia was in bed *hours* ago; and look
what a lovely rosy complexion she has.")

Celia was now busy counting the cherry stones arrayed
round the edge of her plate, touching each one with her
spoon. One or two slipped off and made a stain on the
cloth, but no one rebuked her.

"This year, nex' year, sometime, nev – oo, Mummy,
give me another one quick, or it'll come out never!"

"You'll never learn manners, that's right," I said nastily.

"Pooh to you, smarty!"

"Children, children!" said my mother, as though I were
seven years old too.

"You are both – er-urp! Celia, go and fetch Daddy the
bicarbonate of soda."

After I had helped to wash up, I went out into the
twilit garden where blackbirds were going to roost with an
agitated chattering. A late magpie flew overhead, sawing
the air with impatient wings. There was a scent of flowers
– wallflowers, chrysanthemums – which filled me with melancholy, a nostalgia for some forgotten home of the spirit.

I didn't in the least regret my decision about not taking
on the new Thursday women's pages. Editing them would
mean arranging full-page spreads of glossy fashion prints;
and sitting all day in a dark inside room by a light-well,

like Roma who did the women's section of the Weekend Magazine.

It wasn't Life, it wasn't real. I longed for involvement with real life.

My friend Roma said it was all meaningless anyway, so what matter whether you wrote fashion notes or classical novels since it would be all the same in a few thousand years' time. "You take things too seriously, Mal," she would lecture me. "Relax and enjoy life, why don't you?"

I walked past the side of the house and the garage, from which my father's car had disappeared long ago, and which now housed Mr Hackett's gleaming sedan. My own car, when I bought it, would have to stand out in the weather.

Well at least Mother wasn't opposing the idea of a car, even if she couldn't be counted on for much support. She was very easy-going except for odd occasions when she seized on some idea and kept to it against all arguments, with an obstinacy that used to infuriate her first husband. ("Your mother's pig-headedness", he used to call it.)

I'd half expected her to raise objections on the grounds of safety. There were so many car accidents these days, and after all my father had been killed in one . . .

A thought which had been floating just beneath my consciousness now came to the surface, exploding almost audibly like a bubble in boiling mud. I stopped dead, my eyes fixed on the afterglow in the west.

Repair bills! That was the phrase which, ever since dinner, had set up the disturbance that had been churning around in my subconscious mind.

There had apparently been no repairs necessary to my father's car after the accident, and that was odd now I thought about it. It had been there in the garage when I came home from Aunt Flora's after a few days, and I couldn't remember that it was knocked about. My father was a good driver, and had looked after it well.

I began walking on slowly, out of the gate and down to the corner from where I could see the lights winking on in the city. From this distance the square buildings looked like cardboard cut-outs against a sheet of orange paper.

I knew that accidents bad enough to kill a man usually left their mark on a car. It was very strange.

I leaned on a picket fence and watched the first faint stars appear. There was not a cloud in the sky; it was clear and luminous as water.

That fateful morning the sky had been like this, un-marred by a single cloud. We were having a geography lesson out of doors, after the long holiday weekend. I was looking across at Dinah whose fair skin was sunburnt to a bright pink which clashed with her yellow plaits.

There was a step on the gravel; I turned idly to watch the big girl approaching with the message that was to upend my world.

"Marigold Trent," said Miss Moody, "Miss Titchfield wishes to see you in her study."

With galloping heart and jelly legs I walked through the cold, echoing hall paved with tiles that suggested a prison courtyard. I knocked on the dread door.

And then, what a surprise! Old Titch actually put an arm round me and led me gently to a chair, and was murmuring something about being a brave girl, and that as my mother needed me I could go home straight away, and a taxi was coming for me. There had been an accident . . .

It was some time before I understood that this unwonted camaraderie was due to the fact that my father was dead, so that I was set apart from ordinary girls whose fathers stayed respectably alive.

Like all schoolgirls I dreaded being "different". I slunk back to the classrooms like a criminal to get my straw hat and my case. I had not yet understood except with the surface of my mind.

When I got home Aunt Flora was there, trying to look solemn but with a self-important gleam in her pale eyes.

"You'd better go in and see your mother," she said. "Try to comfort her."

Mother was sitting in her darkened bedroom, a handker-chief balled in one fist, her eyes overflowing. "It's Daddy, dear," she said huskily as I flung myself on to her lap. "He's–he's had an accident. He had an accident and was killed."

"No! I don't believe it!" I shouted, and burst into tears.

Now, as I remembered, tears rose again to my eyes. A planet glowing among the orange light in the west blurred and trembled, then shot out beams of light like silver spears.

Four

On the day when the Melbourne Cup was to be run, I drew the favourite in the office sweep.

To my disgust I was sent out just before the race was run, to write-up for the *Standard* the preparations for the monster fête in the Baptist Union hall. And as Baptists didn't approve of gambling, I thought glumly, there would be no chance of hearing a broadcast there.

While an enthusiastic organiser was taking me round, I noticed how the workmen preparing the hall (and presumably not Baptists) began fading away; first the men who were hammering at a large wooden stall, then two painters who had been working from a scaffolding on the stage. As soon as I could, I made my escape.

Outside it was as if a plague had struck the city. A few trams still ran, but there was scarcely a car, a van or a pedestrian moving in the streets. Fruitstalls were left unguarded, owners had deserted their paper-stands. Every radio and music-shop had an amplifier going, and round these dense crowds were gathered. They were already beginning to break up, however, the race was over.

I dashed up the stairs to the office trying without

success to take four at a time. At the door of the reporters' room I was greeted by loud cheers. My horse had won. I put the roll of notes unbelievingly into my bag.

The usual thing was for the winner to shout a drink for everyone at the Black Bull, but they let me off because I was a girl.

"You'll have to celebrate, though. What about coming up to the South for a drink?" said a voice behind me.

I disengaged myself from Roma's congratulatory embrace and turned, while my cheeks grew pink. Was this the aloof, the handsome, the sarcastic Mr Ryan addressing me? A god-like Sub-Editor from that small Olympus beside the composing room? The very thought of drinking alone with him at the city's most exclusive hotel terrified me.

Treading hard on Roma's foot, I said, "You see, Mr Ryan, Roma and I were going – "

"Then both come. The company of *two* lovely girls," he said with an ironic bow, "will be twice as pleasant as that of one."

"Oh! We – well, thank you. Shall we, Roma?"

"If you like, Mal."

Seated in the hotel's softly-lighted lounge, my feet sinking into luxurious and loudly-patterned carpet, I began to feel quite elated as I drank a brandy cruster from a pink sugar-rimmed glass. It was, I thought, too pretty to be very strong.

I shouted a second round of drinks from my winnings. Jed Ryan laughed as the waiter faded away with a baffled look.

"Innocence is its own defence!" he said to Roma. "She just didn't know she ought to tip him."

"Oh, *should* I have? Oh dear!"

Roma was looking very *chic* in a black dress with a white collar, and a little black velvet hat like an artist's beret. Catching sight of myself in the mirror-panelled wall, I decided that I would never wear this mouse-brown outfit again. Tomorrow I would buy a slinky black dress and a small black hat that would show most of my red – no, auburn curls. I took one of Jed's cigarettes and smoked it inexpertly.

After the second drink the others seemed to me very witty; we all laughed a great deal. I felt elated. This was Life. And suddenly I was no longer nervous of Jed Ryan. He was singing, quietly and solemnly, a little ditty about Abdul the Bulbul Emir.

Then Roma, who had a dinner date, said that she must go. She seemed to expect me to accompany her, but I rather resented Roma's attempts to be protective from the vantage point of her extra four years and was wilfully dense. When she was gone, Jed leaned towards me.

"I know a little pub in the hills," he said, looking into my eyes, "where you can get the most wonderful fillet steak in the Southern Hemisphere. Care to try it?"

"I should think that in Argentina –" I said in a fuddled way, but found that I was already being propelled towards the door. His hand on my arm sent a tremor of happiness through me. Really, he had the most astounding light-green eyes. Hypnotic, almost. I floated down the stairs without seeming to touch more than one or two.

"My car's round at the garage," he said. "Rather a long walk, but I was getting the brakes fixed."

"Well . . . is it safe?"

"Terribly safe. The safest car in the Southern Hemisphere," he laughed. "Come on."

Outside it was unexpectedly night. I had the sensation of being in a play. Act II, Scene i: Evening. A city street . . .

The tall buildings, bright with lights where the army of cleaners worked, were unreal and illusory as cardboard scenery.

He took my arm as we crossed the street and walked to the car. Then we drove towards the hills whose rounded outlines showed dark against the sky, like the breasts of some giant Ethiopian queen.

*   *   *

Far away below us the city lights sparkled as though that queen had flung down all her jewels. Green, white, red and amber, in rope and necklace and diadem, they ended in the dark blank line of the coast where a lighthouse winked rhythmically its warning spark.

I leant close to the windscreen and felt happiness rise like a bubble in my throat. We had found the little pub in the hills, a low, rambling place with a deserted dining-room. We had a cold beer while we waited for the steak, and a bottle of the local burgundy with the steak when it came.

I thought that Jed knew I would have been shy in the big ornate dining-room of the South Australian, and that it was thoughtful of him to bring me here. It did not occur to me that it was also much cheaper.

Now, rather dizzy with the beer and the burgundy combined with the altitude, I looked out across the lights and felt that I was in a plane just coming in to land from some far, romantic city. Jed turned with one arm along the seat-back and contemplated my profile: my burnished, springy curls. He carefully put out his cigarette.

"You're a pretty wonderful girl, you know," he said . . . And a few minutes later, "I'd better take you home, I suppose."

But I didn't want to go home. I wanted to spend some of my winnings; I wanted to go to the Blue Lagoon, I had never been in a real night-club.

"I just want to see it," I said.

Jed smiled indulgently. "All right."

He kissed me again before turning on the headlights.

On the way down the curving road I was swung against his shoulder on the bends. I looked up at his dark face in the glow of the dashboard light.

"I can't believe I'm really here with you, like this."

He chuckled. "You didn't think my interest in you was purely paternal, did you?"

35

"I didn't think you were interested at all. I was just simply terrified of you, that's all."

"Poor little Marigold. I did bark at you a few times, didn't I? But it was nothing personal. Just trying to make a good journalist out of you. Cubs ought to be terrified."

"Then you shouldn't have spoilt the effect by bringing me up here and . . . and –"

"And proving myself a mere, weak male? Well, I am. But please believe I didn't plan all this when I asked you to come and have a drink. I was lonely. I didn't want to go home to an empty house."

"You're not married, are you?"

"Who told you that?" His voice was teasing.

"Nobody, but – I mean, you wouldn't have asked me."

"Oh, what an innocent! So you think a married man would never go out with anyone but his wife?"

"I didn't say that." I was beginning to feel cross. "I meant you wouldn't be lonely."

"No, you're right." He sighed sharply. "My wife left me, years ago."

"Oh, I'm sorry! But how could she have? I mean –"

He laughed at the naïve, implied compliment.

"I'm not easy to live with, I suppose. You know what a sarcastic beggar I can be."

"I think you're very nice."

"You're sweet."

He kissed my hand, his eyes on the road.

The band was playing wearily, as though their day's work had not just begun. The tired drummer looked as if the sticks would fall at any moment from his nerveless fingers. A solitary couple gyrated between the tables.

Gazing round at the luxurious, mysterious blue velvet curtains, and back at the bubbles in my hollow-stemmed glass, I felt giddy with joy; this was the ultimate haunt of sin and sophistication. Here I was, not yet eighteen, drinking sparkling Hock in a night-club with a terribly handsome man, a divorced man, of more than thirty.

Jed watched me indulgently while I ate an asparagus omelette and sipped my wine, chattering all the time. More couples drifted in. Jed and I danced. I stopped suddenly with a stricken face.

"I forgot! I simply must ring Mother and tell her where I am. She'll think I've gone to Roma's to tea, but if I'm not home soon they'll have the Vice Squad looking for me."

I used a telephone on the wall behind the blue curtains. The bubbles of the wine seemed to have got into my head; I had some trouble with the number. My stepfather's voice came over the wire at last. I realised that the sound of the danceband would drift through the mouthpiece – no use pretending. "Dad, it's me, I'm at the –"

"You'll have to speak up, Marigold, I can't hear a word."

"I'm at the Glue Balloon," I shouted.

"Come here, it's Marigold," I could hear him calling agitatedly. "She's at some dreadful place!"

My mother's calm voice replaced his, and I explained that I would be late, and where I was ringing from.

"But whom are you with, dear?"

I pretended not to hear. "It's perfectly all right. There are only about four people here, and they are most respectably eating Lobster Mornay."

"You're to be home by midnight, do you hear?"

"Yes! Yes! Goodnight."

I went back to the table, eyes sparkling with mischief. "My Pop nearly had a fit, but it's all right."

We danced again. I leaned back and watched the ceiling revolve. "'At the still point of the turning world . . .' Have I had too much to drink?" I wondered giddily, then I ceased to wonder or to care.

I heard with vague surprise Jed remarking that I had beautiful eyes and a flawless complexion . . . and, by some transition that I failed to grasp, that he had a collection of early editions he would like me to see . . . Australiana . . .

When Roma came in with her current escort it seemed absolutely right; the perfect finish to this magical evening.

"There's Stan!" I cried. "Hi, Stan! Come and join us. . . . That's Bob Crossland with her."

"I can't follow this," said Jed, who looked none too pleased. "Which is Stan?"

"Roma, of course. I often call her Stan."

Roma was inspecting me rather oddly, I noticed. She had quite a grim look, and scarcely spoke to Jed. When she led me to the door marked "Ladies" I meekly followed.

"Really, Mal!" Roma rounded on me as soon as we were inside. "You shouldn't be allowed out without a keeper! How much have you had to drink? And what are you doing here with Jed Ryan? I thought you were going straight home from the South."

"We had dinner in the hills," I said, raising my eyes from a fascinated contemplation of a terrazzo floor that heaved in gentle waves like the sea.

"Oh, no! What happened? Quickly!"

"Nothing happened quickly. He kissed me, quite chastely . . . and he kissed my hand. That's all."

Roma relaxed a little. "Not a false move; I see. My dear girl, don't you know the reputation he's got? Don't you know his wife divorced him. Has he mentioned your eyes yet?"

"He said I had beautiful eyes." I sighed sentimentally.

"Ha! That sort begin at your eyes and work down. Has he asked you home with him?"

"He did mention some books he wanted me to see on the way home – rare, r'markable editions."

"Huh, no etchings?"

"He probably has etchings. I'm sure he's very artistic."

"You're coming home with us, my girl. You're in no fit state –"

"I'm perfectly fit, my dear Roma," I said with elaborate dignity, "to – oh! I don't think I feel very well."

Next day I felt very much worse; my mother, with an uncanny sense for what would be most repulsive, gave me a lightly-done egg for breakfast and watched with an eagle eye till it was consumed.

I felt no better after a stern and lengthy lecture from Roma; for, having been goaded at last to an exasperated, "Oh, shut up!" I bounced into the corridor and almost into Jed Ryan, who gave me a frosty smile and a cool "Good-morning, my dear."

His expression was pained; it said that he had no time for immature girls who couldn't trust their own judgement, or him. He passed on his Olympian way towards the Subs' Room.

Feeling very young and crushed, I went round to my desk and opened the morning paper.

Instantly I brightened. There was a whole page of advertisements of very slinky black dresses, and I still had some of my winnings left, though I had insisted on spending some at the night-club.

I saw myself in form-fitting black, with exotic earrings and a cigarette in a long holder, looking with exquisite boredom at a row of first editions:

"Very interesting, my dear Jed," I murmured . . .

The plane trees on North Terrace clapped their leaves like hands in the hot dry wind. Long shadows of tree-trunks lay on the pavement, and the blue sky seemed all the bluer for a few wisps of wind-teased cloud, fine and crinkled as triple-A pure Merino wool.

Pausing at the glass swing-doors of the *Standard* office before climbing the marble stairs to the Literary Department, I lifted my nose like a pointer to the exciting scent of the land breeze which seemed to bring the vast dry continent into the city. Paddocks of ripening wheat, miles of mallee scrub, eucalyptus-scented bush, and red sand – I could smell them all, could almost see, beyond the ring of hills, the wide plains where mirages wavered, kangaroos leapt, and the red dust rose in whirlwind towers.

"I will lift up mine eyes unto the hills," I said, "from

whence cometh my help. My help cometh from the earth . . ."

Out there, exciting things were happening; men were finding gold and opal, mounted police followed the tracks of perishers wandering in circles among the spinifex, Aborigines went walkabout, drovers lived on the edge of danger.

Out there, life was real . . .

Mr Parfitt called me in and told me to go to Marshall's, the largest store, and turn in a puff-par on their new Beauty Salon.

I was disgusted. A "puff-par" is the lowest form of journalism, a tie-up with advertising, the length depending on the amount of paid advertising on the same subject.

"But I have an interview at eleven, Mr Parfitt," I objected.

"I can't help that," he said calmly. "This is important. It's got to go in an early page for tomorrow. They've taken a full-page spread." He rubbed his dark curls slowly with one hand, on which was a gold signet-ring. "About ten inches will do."

"Couldn't someone from the Social staff do it? It's women's page stuff."

"No. They want someone who can write. Let yourself go like you do on those Art Gallery pieces sometimes. I told 'em you were good at that descriptive stuff."

I stamped out, biting furiously on a pencil, and spat out several chips. But as I walked along the Terrace, there were the jacaranda trees already in bloom outside the Public Library, dropping their blue flowers in a ring on the green lawns. I forgot my bad mood, trying out phrases: *The dark trees stand in sea-blue pools, their fallen flowers garlanding the grass* . . . Or *petals*, perhaps – too much alliteration?

The Advertising Manager at Marshall's was oilily affable. I didn't like him, or the way he leered at my legs, which were long and among my good points.

"I bet you wear out a fair few stockings in your job," he said.

"Yes, why?"

"I'll get you a couple of pairs of fully fashioned silk stockings. We want this article to be a good one."

"Thank you, don't bother," I said coldly. "It *will* be good."

The beauty expert, newly arrived from overseas, was so enthusiastic about the new salon, the polished panelling and the gold-plated taps, that she soon had me enthusiastic too.

"Now we weel give *Madame* a sample facial," she said.

"Oh no, I don't –" But I found myself thrust into a long, comfortable reclining chair, my head being swathed in paper bandages, masses of cold cream being smoothed on my face.

"*Madame*'as a nice fine skin, but a leetle dry. All Australian women 'ave the dry skins, it ees the climate."

She spoke hypnotically while the assistant applied and removed mysterious creams, packs and lotions. When the facial and then the make-up were completed, I sat up and looked at myself in the mirror.

A delicately painted mask looked back at me: new eyes, dark and mysterious, slanting up at the corners; iridescent green lids, and eyelashes stiff with mascara; black-pencilled brows; mouth bright pink and slightly luminous.

I pretended to be delighted, and hurried self-consciously back to the office, where there was an immediate reaction among the boys in the Dogbox.

I slunk into the Social Room, to be greeted by a raucous shout from Myfanwy. "Great God! You look like Cleopatra."

"I feel like Jezebel."

"You'd better go and wash your face, child, before you get yourself criminally assaulted."

"I'm not going to wash it off. It was free, but I can't bear to waste it."

41

I sat down with my back to the light and began to type.

Myfanwy, a rather mannish figure with an Eton crop, who smoked cigarettes in a long holder jammed between her formidable teeth, scorned make-up. Her only concession to femininity was to dust some pale Rachel powder over her withered cheeks, which gave her rather a ghastly air till it wore off.

She would have nothing to do with a typewriter, but wrote her copy flowingly in a beautiful script. She had a beaming smile, revealing all of her crooked teeth, for those – mostly women – that she did not like. Her real smile was a little humorous quirk of the lips. I was honoured that she never turned the public smile on me.

The only other occupant of the Social Room was Helen Mayne, a quiet girl, soft voiced and reserved, who was completely under the domination of Myfanwy.

My story on the beauty salon appeared next day as a news item, with nothing to indicate that hundreds of pounds worth of advertising was behind it.

While it was printing I went up to the roof, feeling the thunder of the presses in the base of the building like the throb and pulse of blood through my own arteries. The great presses whirled round in the pride of their power, the ribbons of paper streamed past in a blur of black and white.

I walked out on to the roof and leaned on the sun-warm stone of the parapet. Far below, the dark hurrying specks of people moved up and down and across, in apparently aimless motion. Cars, buses, bicycles and trucks came and went. Trains shunted in the railway yards.

All this movement and activity – it was like the top of a boiling pot, like the restless motion of a fire, the rippled surface of the sea. A manifestation of energy, no more.

For the moment I stood detached and looked down at life. But by my own breathing, by the warmth of the sun felt on my hands as they rested on the stone, I knew that I too was a part of it, inescapably.

Inescapably? I had only to let myself drop down there –
a simple movement, over in seconds – to be out of it all
forever.

I drew back from the edge, amazed at myself. Who
would wish to die? I left the roof and wandered downstairs
again while, behind me, the afternoon burnt out in smoky
rose.

Five

As the summer advanced my face became paler with the heat until, according to my stepfather, my eyes looked like two burnt holes in a blanket. Instead of turning a fashionable tan, I came out in a crop of freckles.

Made beauty-care conscious by my visit to the Marshall Salon, I invested in some false eyelashes, jade green eyeshadow, and a bottle of some miraculous face pack that was supposed to remove freckles in one simple operation, entirely harmless to "all but the most sensitive skins".

This last phrase sounded a little ominous; how did you know whether your skin was sensitive or not until you tried the stuff on it? But it was worth trying, for I was going out with Sandy Martin tonight and I wanted to dazzle him.

I washed my hair and while it was drying went to get the face-pack from where it was hidden among my underthings in a drawer. This was necessary because one of my mother's prejudices was against things in bottles, many of which, she believed, could maim, blind or cause all the hair to fall out.

I delved for the tissue-wrapped pink carton but when I

44

opened it the bottle was half empty. "Frauds," I muttered, unscrewing the cap. I took out the little brush that went with it and painted the queer-smelling thick white stuff over my face, leaving only a space round my eyes and a thin area of lips showing.

As I peered at my reflection in the mirror I felt almost afraid of my own face. There was something hateful about it, with thin lips and dark slits of eyes in a pale, unhealthy-looking mask.

A sudden thump on the door, which crashed open, made me jump.

"I wish you wouldn't burst in like that, Celia!" I snapped. "I've told you and told you to knock before you enter a lady's bedroom."

"'Tisn't a lady's bedroom, it's only yours." Celia tossed her dark curls, conscious of her picture-book prettiness as she looked past me into the mirror. "Oo, you've got stuff on your face. Mum-mee! Marigold's got –"

"SHUT UP!" I said so fiercely that Celia jumped.

"You *do* look awful!" she said.

"Yes, but you wait till I wash this mask off. It –"

"But that's the stuff I put on my doll's face –"

"You little beast!" I made a swipe at her with the hair-brush, but missed. "So that's why the bottle was half empty! D'you know what this stuff costs? Fifteen-and-six!"

"But I put it on my doll's face, and her face all melted," said Celia.

"What!" I looked anxiously at the white mask in the mirror. It had now set like plaster of Paris.

Did I feel a burning sensation beneath the mask? Was my face being eaten away? With a yell of terror I flew to the bathroom and bathed the horrid stuff off with warm water.

My skin was rather red, but did not seem to be actually coming off.

Back in my room I found Celia using my new lipstick. I snatched it from her and pushed her out of the door. I dressed, then made up my face with the utmost care, the way they had done it at Marshall's, and then glued on the false eyelashes. This was a lot more difficult than I'd expected, and took a long time. Sandy would be here any minute.

I posed in front of the mirror with my tinted lids drooped languorously, my lashes sweeping my cheek. I looked down my nose with ineffable disdain, looked up invitingly beneath my brows, smiled and tossed my head. Perhaps it was just the powder over them but my freckles did seem to have faded, and my skin glowed.

Should I ask Mother for the loan of her turquoise ear-rings? She had been rather reluctant to lend anything since I had borrowed, and lost, her best pearl brooch.

"Marigold!" It was my mother, psychic as ever. "Where are you going tonight?" She coughed in the scented mist of powder drifting into the passage.

I opened my door, keeping my back to the light. "Out," I said repressively.

"Yes, but where, and who with?"

"With Sandy Martin."

"Well, see you're home by midnight. Don't forget you have to be at work tomorrow. I'll be waiting up for you."

"Oh Mother! Do you *have* to?"

"I'll be awake, anyway."

The telephone rang in the hall. I darted to answer it, sure it was for me. It was Sandy; his Special had just blown up, and his father was out in his car, so we would have to put it off until another night.

"Oh Sandy!" I couldn't help sounding reproachful; he would mess about with his car and alter its insides all the time.

"What about – perhaps you could borrow –?" he suggested.

"I'll try. Hold on."

Forgetting about my face, I rushed into the sitting-room

46

where Mr Hackett was quietly burping to himself behind the evening paper.

"Dad, could I borrow your car? Just this once? Please?"

"What for?" He lowered the paper and looked at me suspiciously.

"To go out, of course. With Sandy. His car – it won't start."

"I'm not surprised at that. Where were you going?"

"Just out."

"Then I don't see the urgency –" He tilted his head back to bring the high-powered lower half of his bifocals to bear on my agitated face. "Marigold! What have you done to your eyes? Mother, come and look at this!"

In a moment they were both staring at my glamorised face.

"You look like a – a – streetwalker!" cried my stepfather at last, pulling this quaint old-fashioned term out of the depths of his memory. "And you're certainly not going out in my car looking like that."

"In fact you'd better not go out at all," said Mother.

I stormed and argued, but it was no good once they joined forces, and I knew it. I went back to the phone and told Sandy, between sobs of frustration.

"I say, you're not crying are you?" he asked anxiously.

"No, of course not! But aren't parents mad? It's so stupid it's funny, really." I laughed hysterically, and hung up. Then I went to bed and cried into my pillow, getting streaks of green eyeshadow over it. The eyelashes hurt as I pulled them off.

"What a waste!" I sobbed. "What a fearful, frightful waste!"

All my careful make-up had done was upset my stepfather's delicate digestion. I could hear him, when I stopped crying, shadow-boxing in the hall in an effort to dispel his discomfort. There was a thumping of feet, a jingle of coins in his pockets, then a yell of pain followed by a crash.

47

I guessed rightly that he had collided with the latest of Mother's "floral arrangements", a large jar of purple-flowered wild artichokes, which she insisted were Scotch thistles and very decorative, and which were covered with vicious spines. The last thing I heard before dropping off to sleep was the front door being opened and the bronze jar being cast outside with considerable force.

The very next week I invested in "Strawberry", so called because her paintwork was of a faded crushed-strawberry pink which once, long ago, had been red. Her wheels had a knock-knee'd appearance and she gave out clouds of blue smoke. I thought she was beautiful.

"It looks like a heap of junk to me," said my stepfather, pointing out that parts of the engine were tied together with bits of wire. "Second-hand cars are nothing but an expense. But they who will not be counselled, cannot be helped."

"Strawberry has personality," I explained. "You can't get disc wheels like that today. She's a most unusual little car."

"Most unusually decrepit," he said crisply.

My mother said nothing but, "It seems a nice little car for the money." She made no objections on the grounds of safety in spite of its rather dangerous appearance. Why wasn't she nervous about car accidents? Unless, when her first husband was killed, it was no accident.

A fantastic suspicion grew, fed by my ever fertile imagination. How long had she known Mr Hackett? How much had he wanted to marry her? My father had stood in the way . . .

Oh no, I thought, horrified at the way my thoughts were running. Such things did not happen. Yet they did, they happened all the time; but not to mild, middle-aged people like Mr and Mrs Hackett. The idea of them feeling passionately about anything but food was ludicrous.

A new thought surfaced from the dark and jumbled mass that had been churning round in my brain. It was what Mr Muecke had said at the Art Gallery, "It was a sad business when he –" and then he'd stopped and made a great business of locking up the showcase.

"Let's hope she never knows the whole story, poor kid!" – Aunt Flora's voice.

I felt a burning desire to know. I felt sure, by now, that something had been hidden from me, and I was beginning to imagine things that might be worse than the truth.

I drove up to the hills to brood over the problem undisturbed. Parking in the curve of a disused quarry, I began to climb the steep hillside above. The short brown turf was ringed with the grazing-tracks of sheep. Dark pellets of sheep-dung rolled from under my feet as I climbed towards the sky.

Soon the tops of the trees were foaming and hissing in the wind that was yet cut off from me by the curve of the hill. I kept my head down, climbing steadily. Then the wind caught me a solid buffet in the chest. I was there.

I felt myself grow light, expanding like a gas to fill the wide prospect. Fold upon fold of smooth gold-grassed hills fell away to the level plain. Sunlight picked out a window in the suburbs, a green playing field, a wisp of smoke. Beyond lay the pale blue band of Spencer's Gulf, in whose sheltered waters I had learned to swim with my real father. He was a good swimmer, and had taught me in a day.

Yet after he died we ceased to visit the beach on weekends, though it was only ten miles away. I had never ventured very far out, even after I became a confident swimmer, because at the back of my mind was the memory of what had happened to Uncle Fred. Every long bank of brown seaweed looked like a possible shark. I swam always with my eyes rolling uneasily round me, or I kept to very shallow water. To reinforce my fear, a few years later a young woman, a champion swimmer, dived off the jetty at another suburban beach almost into the jaws of a twelve-foot White Pointer.

That gruesome death must have made a front-page story for the *Standard*. I imagined how Mr Smythe's steel-grey eyes would have gleamed at the headlines. Dog Bites Man might not be news, but Shark Bites Man – or Woman – was rare enough to rate a 48-point head at least.

Gazing at the innocent-looking sea, its blue as frail and delicate as a flower, I thought again of my strong father and his arms supporting me in the water.

Although we never spoke of it, I resolved to ask Mother about my father's death as soon as an opportunity arose. But Mother and I could never talk to each other except about the most superficial things; and of course I kept putting it off.

Six

"I have to go out for half an hour, dear," said Myfanwy, winding a scarf round her withered throat and dusting some flour on her face in front of the small mirror. "Just keep an eye on things for me till Helen gets back, will you?"

"Right."

But when she had gone I scowled after her. "You will be treated as a man, Miss Trent. Ha-*ha*."

I banged out some Personals on the typewriter. A timid knock at the door, and a large, beefy, black-haired woman edged round it, drawing after her a bashful younger edition of herself.

"Me daughter's getting married," she said, and stopped expectantly as if she had just announced the most world-shaking event since the relief of Mafeking.

"Yes, and Queen Anne's dead," I nearly answered, but managed a polite, "Oh, yes?"

"Yes. We'd like 'er pitcher in the paper."

She produced a shiny studio-portrait and laid it reverently on the table. It bore some resemblance in general outline to her daughter; but the cheeks had been visibly thinned by a process of scraping, two glittering highlights had been gouged in the dull eyes, the mouth had been redrawn in a perfect Cupid's bow, and long dark lashes had been pencilled in.

It was hideous, and I knew Myfanwy wouldn't use it in a thousand years.

"Well . . . I'm afraid I can't promise. We have so little space, you see." I tried the beaming, falsely genial smile Myfanwy used on hopeless cases. The mother remained unmoved.

"We'd like 'er pitcher in the paper. We alwus buy the *Standard*."

"Yes, well, just leave it and I'll see what can be done. The Social Editress is out at present."

"And what about a reporter at the wedding?"

Much hope, I thought. Now, if it was Greta Garbo marrying the Prince of Wales . . . I fetched one of the regular printed forms from a drawer. "If you'll just fill in the details, and post it back not later than Wednesday morning . . . The wedding's on Saturday, I suppose?"

"Yes. Doris is 'aving four bridesmaids and a little flowergirl."

Erkh, I thought. "Well, there are printed headings for all those things. Just fill in the spaces and post it in. There you are. Good morning."

"But will there be a reporter?"

Here the bashful daughter, who had not said a word, plucked at her parent's arm. "Come *on*, Mum!" They disappeared round the corner.

I recorded the new, strange and interesting fact that Mr George H. Pratt, manager of Fast-Fix Zipp Fasteners Ltd, had arrived in the Overland express and was staying at the Botanic Hotel.

Yet exciting things were happening everywhere. Everywhere, I felt, except in this particular city and on my particular round.

This very week I had stumbled on a story, not world-shaking but at least newsworthy, and I couldn't print it because that beast Dr Greeley, the Medical Superintendent at the Prince George Public Hospital, wouldn't give me confirmation. Getting facts from him was always like extracting burrs from wool.

Noel Richards, the Med. student I sometimes went out with, was in his final year which meant being a resident at the Hospital; and he had told me on Saturday night that the Radiology department would shortly be acquiring a new X-ray plant from Germany, very up-to-date and meaning a large expenditure of public money.

Each day I had to visit the hospital's Casualty ward to get the records of the latest accidents and admissions, and to check with Switchboard on the condition of critically ill victims.

Just inside the main door sat "Switch" before a bewildering array of plugs and wires. She was a thin alert young woman, who pulled out plugs, flicked down switches, and talked into the mouthpiece near her chin in the same laconic voice, even when she was giving life-or-death replies to anxious relatives.

She had a series of roneoed foolscap sheets with the names of patients, and beside each name the fateful words: Serious . . . condition critical . . . unchanged . . . satisfactory . . . improving.

"Switch" kept a roll of knitting in her meagre lap, so there must have been times when she was not busy.

"Dr Greeley will see you now," she said out of the side of her mouth to me. "Hullo? Switchboard. *Switch*-board. What ward, please? One moment . . ."

I went along the corridor with a heart that was sinking like soggy plum-pudding. I didn't like Dr Greeley, and Dr Greeley hated the Press. They were always sending me to ask him for comments (known to Editor's Conference as "follow-ups") on fantastic cures and strange devices, usually originating in the USA or the Soviet Union. His

53

views consisted always of a cynical disbelief; and he was a busy man.

I had often suffered under his sarcasm. Though I thought the questions just as silly as he did, it was my job to ask them, and I thought it unfair to take out his annoyance on-me. I passed the door marked MATRON and came to the one marked MEDICAL SUPERINTENDENT. Tucking my hair nervously behind my ears, I knocked, took a deep breath, and went in, trying to look bold and carefree. Timidity only made him worse.

"Sit down, young woman," he said rapidly. "I'm very busy, I've no time to waste on the latest miracle-cure for cancer claimed in the USSR. What wild rumour is your office pursuing now?"

His small, bilious, intelligent eyes with their puffy underlids looked at me coldly. His skin was pasty and unhealthy-looking, his mouth a thin line. He reminded me of how I'd looked with the Freckle-Remover on my face – hateful.

Trying to keep the dislike out of my voice, I said, "It's nothing like that this time, Dr Greeley. It's just – I heard that the Hospital was getting a new X-ray machine, and I wanted it officially from you."

His black brows came together in a sharp frown. I looked past his smooth, rather reptilian head at the picture on the wall behind his desk: a reproduction of *Bridge at Argenteuil* by Monet. I remembered that the Doctor was interested in art and was said to have a valuable collection of drawings and prints in his home.

"I fail to see," Dr Greeley said icily, "what this has to do with the public."

"But it's news. And it is public money that is being spent."

"I have nothing to say on the matter."

"May I just say that the new plant includes some of the latest equipment available for deep-ray therapy in Europe, and that we will soon have the most up-to-date –"

He glared at me. "Who told you that?"

"Then it is true?"

"It's true we are getting it, but I told you I have NO COMMENT. The usual news bulletin will be issued after the next meeting of the Hospital Board."

"Yes, in the *Recorder's* time. What about the *Standard*?"

"I am equally indifferent, young woman, to both the morning *and* the evening scandal-sheets. Now if you don't mind, I'm busy."

Ungracious bastard, I thought, getting up to go. "If you could just give me an idea of what it will cost – "

He had begun writing, ignoring me. My hands shook so that I dropped a wad of copy-paper, and in bending to retrieve it my eyes came level with a wire in-tray at the back of his desk. In it was a brochure, printed in German, with a picture of a large, complicated-looking mechanism. A figure with many noughts and a £ sign in front of it had been marked in the margin with ink. My head twisted to read it, I felt Dr Greeley's cold eyes looking at me. I picked up the copy-paper and marched out.

He's impossible, he's getting worse and worse, I thought now as I corrected the Personal pars and took them down to the Subs' Room. If only I were quite certain of the details I'd print the story without his consent.

As I came out of the Subs' Room, Roma Richardson came past from the composing room with a sheaf of damp galley proofs flying from her hand like streamers.

"Stan! Have you a minute to spare?" I cried.

"What is it, Mal?"

"Come up to the roof, old girl, I've got something Most Secret to tell you."

"Well . . . all right. I have to make up a page in half an hour, though. And I must correct these proofs. They will only take five minutes."

"I'll come round for you then."

I often wondered how I had stood the office before Roma arrived to take the place of the overwhelmingly smart and efficient former Editress. Roma had large, expressive eyes, sometimes blue and sometimes green, but never sharp. There was something comfortable about her; she was an interested spectator of life, with a slow, deep, unhurried voice like Mr Perceval's. I knew she was inclined to laugh at me for being too intense, for my crush on the Editor and my hatred of Subs who deleted all my best paragraphs; but she laughed with me too, and her sense of humour was infectious.

As I went round to her room five minutes later, a scream – not a shot – rang out. I half expected it to be followed by a "sickening thud". Instead Roma came flying out of her room, her usually smooth dark hair almost on end.

"A cockroach!" she gasped. "A horrid, great cockroach in my files."

She went round to the Dogbox. "Quick, Mr Flannigan, there's a great cockroach in my room. Quick, before it gets away!"

Freddo Flannigan turned his head in a bored fashion and addressed one of the copy-boys:

"Mervyn, take two boys and a dog and remove the dangerous insect from Miss Richardson's room."

"Really, Roma," I said reproachfully. "You gave me a terrible fright. I'd no idea you could move so fast. It's probably very Freudian, this horror of insects."

"It's only insects with *feelers*. I can't bear the way they wave those long whiskers."

"Very Freudian, yes."

"Oh, shut up."

"Anyway, come up to the roof, Stan. I've had a brilliant idea, and you can help. Only you mustn't breathe a *word*."

We went up the narrow stairs.

"Now get it off your chest – such as it is," she said.

I leered at Roma's well-developed bust. "Well, I'd hate to have as much on my mind as you have."

We leaned on the sun-warm stone parapet while I told her I had a story which would scoop the *Recorder* and leave it for dead.

"How nice," said Roma lazily. "Oh, this sun is lovely. But it will make me sleepy, I'm afraid."

"Wake up and listen, will you!" I said, wanting to shake her. "I can't get past Dr Greeley, the Med. Sup. at the Hospital; you know how he hates the Press. But if I could only get hold of that paper on his desk . . . I'm known by sight there of course, but if only you –"

"Me!" cried Roma. "You must be crackers! You're joking, of course. You know how I like a quiet life."

"Yes, I know. Quietly going out with a different man every night . . . Wait, I have it!"

"What, my child?"

"Myfanwy! You know how she loves to gamble. We'll bet her five pounds. Well, I'll bet her five pounds. You lend me two pounds ten until Friday."

"She'd never do it."

"But if we made it a bet! And you know how well she takes off the General Manager, and his secretary? She's in all the Repertory productions. Now if only she . . ." and I outlined my great plan.

Roma at last agreed to put up half the money. I waited for Myfanwy to come in and put the idea to her when Helen was out of the room. I knew she loved a good story, whether low, apocryphal, or authentic; if she carried out my plan, she would have a story which would last her for weeks.

"I'm willing to bet you five pounds you can't do it," I added to put her on her mettle.

"Ha! I could do it all right, my girl, but it's damn risky. I might get gaoled or something."

"But I'd come forward and explain it was all done for a bet."

"Greeley will be furious if I get the dope and you print it."

"Of course, but he won't be able to do much about it. And he couldn't get more unhelpful than he is already. I'll claim 'informed circles' like the political correspondents do."

"God! I hope I don't meet him face to face. Surly beggar – always was."

"Then you'll do it? Hooray! But you must promise not to tell anyone for a week."

"You'll have to look after the Social Room."

"Of course. The Supe makes his round of the wards between ten and eleven – you'll be quite safe then. Matron will be with him."

Myfanwy chewed her cigarette-holder between teeth like rock-crushers. "Hrmph! I hope so . . . I say, did you see that lovely misprint in the *Recorder* this morning? 'Mrs Andrew MacTennant in her beige lust-coat . . .' Ha!"

Seven

"All great surgeons have spatulate fingers," said Noel Richards, holding his hand up against the light from the dashboard. "I have spatulate fingers," he added casually.

His other hand held the chunky briar pipe he affected, along with tweedy sports coats with leather patches on the elbows. We were parked in my stepfather's car on the banks of the Torrens (an artificial lake fed by a very small stream, which was named in the early days after a local dignitary).

I had rung Noel and offered to call for him this evening, because I wanted to pick his brains about Radiology and X-ray therapy. But as I turned in the gate on my way home, one of Strawberry's chronically wobbling wheels had fallen off, so I had to borrow the family car. This was never easy. I explained that it was necessary for me to go out to get material for an important article I was writing, and so managed to get the car along with many injunctions about driving carefully and being home early.

Noel had just explained that he despised Radiologists, who were only glorified photographers, while surgeons held life and death in their hands.

"The Radiologist," I pointed out, "interprets X-ray plates so that the surgeon knows where, and whether, to operate."

"Oh yes, he has his uses of course," said Noel loftily. He tamped down tobacco with a well-manicured finger. "If you want the latest dope on X-rays used in radiotherapy for deep-seated tumours and so on, get hold of last June's copy of the *Lancet*."

"And is Dr Greeley particularly interested in radiotherapy? Do you think buying this new equipment was his idea?" (Noel was going to be one of my "informed sources".)

"I should think so. Though the money in my opinion could well have been spent on new quarters for the nursing staff. They live in a kind of dungeon half underground. Have you *seen* their rooms? It's unbelievable."

"No, but you obviously have."

He grinned in the darkness and sucked his pipe until it bubbled. "Well – unofficially, of course. They're strictly out of bounds."

"Dr Greeley wouldn't care how they lived. That man is a soulless machine."

"Sinister-looking bastard, isn't he? But not quite soulless. He's mad about the French Impressionists, hates modern art –"

"He hates newspapers too." I shivered with fear and excitement, thinking of his rage if my plan succeeded.

"Are you cold, my sweet?" Noel put out a long arm and drew me towards him, while carefully depositing his pipe in the glove-compartment at the same time.

"Oh Noel, *please* be sensible. I want to talk to you, I told you."

"It's you who are not being sensible. You know what that bloke Herrick said about 'Gather ye rosebuds while ye may, Old Time is still a-flying'." He brought his other arm into play, and his spatulate fingers began a gentle exploration of my anatomy.

"It's funny, you know," he said dreamily after a while, "how completely different a live body feels. Preserved in formalin a corpse isn't rigid, only a rather odd colour. This year we had a chap called Bertie from the City Morgue to cut up; he had a yellow moustache. I was quite fond of old Bertie."

I shuddered and extricated myself from his embrace.

"Where do you get bodies from for Anatomy?"

"Oh, people who die unidentified at the Hospital. One was a deadbeat fished out of the river. He was probably more useful dead than he'd ever been in life. And others leave their carcasses to the University Med. School."

I looked at the black water, where the lights of the City Bridge were reflected like the ragged yellow petals of drowned chrysanthemums . . . flowers on the grave of a lonely old suicide.

Thoughtfully, Noel kissed my neck. Was he mentally seeing the carotid artery full of red and white corpuscles?

He said, "This car is a bit inhibiting. I suppose your old man isn't going to pop out of the boot?"

I laughed. "No, but I'll have to go in a minute. I promised not to stay out late, and soon he'll start imagining I've smashed up his precious car, and begin ringing the police."

"Gosh, we only just got here," grumbled Noel.

I dropped him at the Hospital gates, resisted the suggestion that I should come up the back stairs for a coffee in his room, resisted the urge to tell him of the great scoop I was planning for the morrow, and drove home singing.

I kept my head well out of the side window and exceeded the speed limit for the sake of the stronger wind in my face and hair.

In the clear night the stars sped on behind the trees, keeping pace however fast I drove. Turning into our street, I slowed abruptly to a moderate twenty miles an hour and coasted into the drive, knowing my stepfather's ears would be strained to catch anything like the crunch of fender on gatepost, or the squeal of brakes suddenly applied.

Next morning, at five minutes to eleven, Myfanwy's small sedan swung away from the front of the *Standard* office with a large-bosomed, square-faced figure at the wheel.

The white nurse's uniform was padded out with two pairs of stockings, Myfanwy's and mine. She wore white cotton stockings and low-heeled white shoes. A scarlet shoulder-cape, insignia of wartime service, finished off her costume, for she had recently played the part of an Army Sister in an amateur show.

Not a detail was out of place. She had changed her horn-rimmed glasses for a gold-rimmed pair like the Matron's, and her Eton crop was hidden under a white veil.

I had drawn a plan of the Med. Sup.'s office, with a window opposite the door, in front of this the desk with the wire basket, and a filing-cabinet at right angles to the wall, behind which she might be able to hide if surprised.

"How do you spell 'incarcerate'?" asked Helen suddenly from across the table.

I jumped. "What an ominous word! Let's hope Myfanwy doesn't get a gaol sentence out of this . . . I, n, c, a, r, c, e, r, a, t, e. She must be there by now."

After half an hour I was biting my pencil to shreds and spitting out pieces of graphite all over the table. What had happened? She should be back by now . . . Dr Greeley would be back from his round of the wards at any minute.

The phone rang. I jumped as though stung, and grabbed the receiver. "Social Room."

"Is that you, Myfanwy?" said a richly Social voice.

"Darling, I wonder if you would do a thing for me? It's just a small piece for today's page —"

"Today's page is already made up, I'm afraid, and Miss Jones is out at present. Can I take the details?"

Impatiently I took down a Social Note about someone's impending holiday in Tasmania, typed it out and put it in the wire basket on Myfanwy's desk. I began pacing the room, which had a faded carpet and two cane chairs to distinguish it from other parts of the office.

"Do sit down, you make me nervous," said Helen.

"Make YOU nervous? What do you think I am? I can't stand this much longer. I'll have to go and see what's happened to her."

Just then I heard the swing-doors open along the corridor. I bounded out and there she was coming towards me — Matron Ferguson to the life. For one dreadful moment I thought it *was* the Matron, come to complain to the Editor about the impersonation.

But she came on to our door and it was Myfanwy, safely back. She collapsed into a cane chair, giggling like a schoolgirl, taking off the gold-rimmed glasses to wipe her streaming eyes.

"God, what a story!" she said when she could speak.

"Myfanwy, you promised!"

"All right, I won't breathe a word, or not for weeks. But if you could just have seen old Greeley's face —"

"He caught you, then!"

"He did not! He came back, though, just as I was finishing taking my notes. I grabbed the pen off his blotter and met him at the door, with the light behind me. 'Just popped in to borrow your pen, Doctor,' I said. 'Mine's rolled away somewhere.' He looked daggers, but he didn't say a word. I dropped the pen at the Matron's door and skedaddled. On the way out I met a young nurse in the corridor and she said 'Good-morning, Matron'."

She handed me an envelope addressed to the Medical

Superintendent as proof. I handed over the five pounds and shook her hand warmly.

"You were certainly game," said Helen. "Marigold says that Dr Greeley is a real horror."

(I imagined a scene where the Doctor, after impatiently going to retrieve his pen and finding the Matron not in, walked on it in her doorway as he was going out again. He bent to retrieve it just as she came back; and the glare he gave her for which the poor woman had no idea of the reason, would simply confirm her opinion that he was a good doctor, but a boor.)

Myfanwy had not been able to find the brochure; but in the out-tray were several letters in carbon, one addressed to a large German manufacturer of scientific equipment. On behalf of the Hospital Board, it accepted their tender for supplying the Hospital with a new X-ray plant for deep therapy, naming a sum which raised her eyebrows.

Beside the blotter lay a copy of the *Lancet*, with an "X" marked against the very article Noel had told me about. She was just taking a note of the date when she heard the doctor's heavy tread in the flagged corridor, and with great presence of mind snatched up his pen.

She handed me her notes and prepared to remove her disguise.

"You're a marvel, Myfanwy," I said.

I sat down at the typewriter to prepare my story for the late edition. I found a filed copy of the *Lancet* in the "morgue", and soon had all the details.

I headed it:

HOSPITAL'S £50,000 FOR NEW PLANT

numbered the pages and took it down to the Subs.

Tension was mounting in their room as the hour of the "death-knock" drew near. The Chief Sub was savagely martyring some unwanted copy on an iron spike. The Cable Editor crouched like a thin spider among his webs of white tape. The teleprinter ticked monotonously to itself in a corner, while a boy waited to tear off the tongue-full of printed news it was jerkily poking into the room.

A compositor came in from the Stone, where pages were made up, with a damp page-proof dangling from his two hands. As I reached the door every head was bent above the big table.

"Marigold!" A savage bark from the Chief Sub.

I turned back. "Why the hell didn't you tell us this was coming in? I'd have held a space on Page One."

"I – I didn't know for sure if I could get it. I've just written it in the last five minutes."

Feeling deflated, and limp from the release of tension, I wandered through the composing room on my way to see Roma on the other side of the building. This huge room, with its hot smells of metal, its feverish clicking and tapping of almost-human linotype machines, its black-fisted compositors in their leather aprons, was always stimulating. Under the blue lights, lipstick turned a weird purple; I wondered what exotic colour my red hair might take on.

In Roma's small room the light burned like eternity, but no one was there. I decided to treat myself to a whole hour off for lunch. There would be no repercussions from the Hospital just yet.

"Good story, Marigold," said the Chief of Staff the next morning. He groped for the cigarette that was smouldering in the ash-tray on his desk. "How'd you drop on to it?"

"Oh – you know. I have my contacts," I said mysteriously.

"Um, yes, well . . ." He seemed about to go to sleep, but woke up to suggest I should see the Director of the

Art Gallery about a forthcoming loan exhibition of modern French painting.

"It's very advanced stuff, should be good for some indignant letters to the Editor from outraged art lovers," said Mr Parfitt. "You might write one yourself to start the ball rolling."

"I could do it with my eyes shut, right now: 'What is the art world coming to, when such senseless daubs, which might have been executed by a colony of monkeys playing with pots of paint, are not only acclaimed but sent around the world . . . ?'"

"Yes; that's the idea."

I found Mr Muecke, always a jolly and extroverted man, in an expansive mood. "This exhibition's really something," he said. "Most exciting stuff we've seen in Australia for years. But come and see something more 'traditional'. It's a David Davies – still down in the vaults – it's not hung yet."

We went down the marble stairs to the vaults where paintings were stacked against walls and in crates, some still in packing-cases, some being restored or reframed and waiting to take their place again in the world above.

The picture leant against a pillar. Its surface seemed to swim with liquid light, each wave made up of dashes of pure colour.

We stood back and looked at it. "*St Ives* – a brilliant piece of work," said the Director. "We were lucky to get it."

"It's beautiful. But I still prefer his *Moonrise*, I think. The colours are so subtle."

"Ah, but you're a Romantic, that's why. Moonlight, and the world well lost –"

"I am not. I intend to marry for money, if at all."

"Nonsense. You'll throw yourself away on the first young man who comes along."

"No; I mean to see Life. And London, Latvia, Labrador

. . . And the blue mosques of Isfahan, and Samarkand, and the Temple of Taormina, and –"

"And 'shining Popocatapetl'! Romantic, as I said –"

I smiled and shook my head.

"–but you'll settle down all right when the time comes."

"Never! I hate the very thought of 'settling down'. I'd become like my mother and my aunt, interested in nothing but food."

He smiled tolerantly. "Youth always thinks it is going to be different."

"And that's another thing! There's no such thing as 'youth', only people. The ones who are young now are growing older every day, and the old ones are dying and new ones growing up. It makes me furious when ministers and members of Parliament talk about 'the Youth of Today' as if we were some great solid mass with only one mind. *Everyone* is different."

"You'd never do in a totalitarian state, my dear. Anyway, come up to my office and I'll give you an advance copy of the catalogue for the exhibition. Now these painters are young in outlook, lively, original – but they're all different! And soon, I suppose, they'll be old-hat, and a new lot will be coming on and being abused by the conservatives. That's life, isn't it?"

"Life is wonderful," I said with conviction. "Can you understand anyone taking his own life? I mean, life is good however bad . . . I just can't *imagine* anyone wanting to commit suicide."

"Er – well, it happens," he said looking at me rather oddly, and led the way upstairs.

The Chief called me in to tell me space was tight, as usual, and to keep it brief. "Oh, and Mr Perceval wants to see you," he added.

All coherent thought flew out of my head, its place taken

by a seething mass of panic. So Dr Greeley was on the warpath already!

I knocked timidly at the Olympian door and went in.

"Ah, Marigold! I wanted to see you. This . . . Dr Greeley at the Prince George Hospital is very annoyed about your article in yesterday's *Standard*. In fact he's furious. He said he never gave you permission to print any information, that he gave you no figures whatever, and wants to know where you got them from. He says he'll dismiss the person responsible when he finds out. I just told him it was our duty to print the news. He didn't deny that the facts were accurate."

"Did you tell him I wrote it?"

"No. We don't give information like that to outsiders. But he particularly asked that no young women with red hair should be sent to interview him again."

A ghost of a twinkle appeared in the Editor's blue eyes.

"Oh dear!"

"How did you get the story, anyway?"

"Well – I have a friend who's a resident, and he has a friend who's a nurse in Radiology . . . and then I saw some papers on the Med. Sup.'s desk, and looked up the rest in the *Lancet*. But Dr Greeley did admit they were getting some new equipment – only he didn't mention the price."

"H'm." Mr Perceval looked judiciously at his pipe. "You know the rule about all information coming from the top in Government departments. Apparently the Board was worried about the sum involved, and wanted to keep it dark for a while. We'll be lucky if we ever get any news from them again."

"It was always like getting blood out of a stone."

"Yes, well, perhaps you'd better keep away from there at present. Good story, though. Scooped the *Recorder*," he said, putting the pipe back in his mouth.

My heart beat high. "So you'll take me off my round and let me do some real reporting?"

"Not just yet. I've no one I could put on your round at present. Besides, you're getting good experience."

I heard the iron finality beneath the friendliness of his tone. He turned to look at a page-proof that had just been brought in.

"Yes, Mr Perceval," I said bitterly, resolving to put in an expense account that would return my five pound bet.

I took a deep breath. "Mr Perceval . . . If I could just have a desk in the Reporters' Room! I hate being in the Social Room, I'm always having to answer the telephone and take Social notes, and they promised me when I started that I would be treated like a man, but they wouldn't ask a man to share a desk with the Social Editress's assistant, and they wouldn't send a man to the Housewives' Association meetings and the National Council of Women and the WCTU . . ."

This was the longest and boldest speech I had ever made in that room, and I waited for the carpet to open and swallow me up. My head reeled.

"Well, now . . ." Mr Perceval stopped to relight his pipe. "I" – puff "– think that might be arranged." Puff. "I'll have a word with the Chief of Staff in the morning."

Noel had given me an idea for another story. I dug up an old school friend who was a trainee nurse at the Prince George (and who incidentally told me that Noel was known as the Wolf of the Wards) and went to see her narrow cell of a room, which was in fact half underground; though it had quite a large window it naturally didn't admit much light.

Then I managed to get the figures on the number of young nurses who had been invalided out because of tuberculosis, and got a nutrition expert to analyse the vitamin content of their meals, all without going through official channels.

When my article appeared, describing the living

quarters, the long hours, the broken off-duty periods, the night-duty without extra pay and the general conditions of the Nurses' Home – which the Chief Architect had originally designed with shower-rooms but no lavatories – there was quite a stir. Questions were asked in Parliament, and the *Standard* was attacked by the Hospital Board. I was rather scared; I avoided the vicinity of the Hospital.

I had moved a short way across the corridor, but a long way in my own estimation. I now had my own desk in the Reporters' Room, with the one disadvantage that the Chief of Staff could watch to see that I was working through the glass partition. But I felt that I was a real reporter at last.

Eight

Mother, who was still in bed, looked over the top of the Sunday paper and said, "Your hair looks nice, dear. Are you going out?"

"Yes, and Sandy is calling for me in about half an hour –"

"Not in that 'home-built contraption' your father objects to?"

"Yes! And I want you to get him out of the front garden until after Sandy gets here. *Please*, Mother; I can't bear it –"

"Well, I'll try. Pass me my dressing gown, and put the kettle on. But you know how obstinate he is," said my mother, herself one of the most obstinate people in Australia.

"Sandy, Sandy, his legs are bandy," chanted Celia, who was lying on the bedroom floor with the comic-strip section.

"Shut up, microbe! No one was talking to you." I rushed off to get ready to make a quick get-away, when I heard Sandy's car in the distance; he was early. It was easy to hear his Special coming. It was famous for the ear-splitting noise of its exhaust, and the number of young men who could be crammed between its doors.

A series of loud explosions sent the dog scuttling under the hydrangeas. I grabbed my bag and hurried outside. My stepfather classed all drivers under twenty-five as "young fools", and would be sure to say something insulting. He particularly disliked ones who called for his daughter. Also he could never distinguish between my escorts and would probably call Sandy "Noel".

He laid down the hedge-shears as I came out. "You see you're home by dark, do you hear?" he said, addressing me but glaring at Sandy. "I don't like you racing around in these home-built contraptions."

"She's quite safe, sir, really," said Sandy. "She won't do more than sixty-five, or seventy downhill –"

"I should hope not!"

I edged quickly out of the gate, drawing Sandy after me. As we coasted off in comparative quietness, he said, "I say, what's biting your old man? He looked as if he'd never seen me in his life before."

"Oh, he thought you were someone else."

He had screwed the windscreen down flat, so that our speed seemed to be doubled. My eyelashes felt as if they would be blown out at the roots. Tears streamed from the outer corner of my eyes.

"I'll never get the tangles out of my hair!" I shouted happily. "Go faster, Sandy!"

As we turned on to the coast road I looked back for speed-cops attracted by the straight-out exhaust, which usually drew them like bees after honey. There was none, but a sleek black Mercedes was overtaking us. In the driver's seat sat Dr Greeley, and he was alone.

"Follow that car!" I shouted as he passed us. "Come on, just for fun. Let's see where he's going."

We dodged in and out of traffic, crossing the white line. "What's that motor-cycle behind? Not the cops, is it?"

"No, no, keep on!"

72

The Doctor's black car was already out of sight round the next bend. Sandy pushed the accelerator flat as we roared past a family of children, travelling backwards in the tray of a utility. I waved; they waved politely back, with doubtful smiles.

We slowed through the township of Booldinga and began to climb the hill beyond. The broad dark-blue band of the sea showed over the yellow wheatfields. The wheat was undulating like water in the wind; the sea was calm as a blue field.

We topped the hill and the landscape opened out like a coloured fan: fallow and ploughland, wheat and stubble, sea and sky.

"Oh . . . !" I cried, "it makes me want to fly!"

I stretched out my arms to embrace it all, and burned the skin off my elbow on the unprotected tyre revolving beside me.

The Special began to make grinding noises. A hot, metallic smell came from under the bonnet.

"She's a bit hot. I'd better stop and let her cool off," said Sandy.

"My elbow hurts!"

"Well, you should keep your arms inside the car, silly."

"What a car!" I said bitterly as we pulled up on the dry grass verge. "Dangerously unprotected, and can't even get up a simple hill."

Sandy flushed to the roots of his dark hair. (He was not sandy-coloured at all; his first name was Alexander.) "Listen, she's been up steeper hills than this with twelve chaps on board. She's a better car than your damn tinny Citroën, anyway. Gutless wonders, they call them."

When we drove on the atmosphere was a little strained, but taking the turn-off to Couriyonga Beach we saw the black Mercedes along a side road, pulled up.

"There it is! Go along there!" I cried.

We cruised along the bumpy secondary road. I peered with interest at the quaint little cottage, all slate roof and overhanging verandahs edged with iron lace. Hesitant smoke was coming from a chimney at the back, as though a fire had just been lit in a wood stove.

"You know whose car that is?" I said. "It's the Med. Sup.'s from the Prince George Hospital. Do you suppose he has a love-nest down here?"

"Snoop!" said Sandy. "What if he has?"

"But I'd love to know! He's such a cold and bloody-minded beast, I can't believe he's half human. And yet –"

I turned and gazed at the cottage till it was out of sight. It was rather picturesque, the sort of thing a doctor with artistic leanings might buy for a weekend retreat.

We paused for a moment at the top of the cliffs to admire the sweep of sea, the dramatic drop to the ochre rocks below, then drove round and down to the beach. We skimmed along the firm sand close to the water's edge. I closed my eyes and pretended we were in a very fast boat setting out for the horizon.

A demon of restlessness possessed me lately. It was worst after I'd been sent to meet a mailboat at the Outer Harbour; one arrived every week, and since anyone who had been abroad or came from overseas was automatically and naïvely considered "interesting", I was supposed to interview passengers from the purser's list.

This I hated, but oh! the towering ship, with its long lighted humming corridors filled with the stuffy, indescribable smell of an overseas liner! The tiers of cabins spilling luggage into alleyways, the coiling pipes, the hot, airless, exciting atmosphere of imminent departure . . . I would long to stow away on board, even though I knew she was only going to another port around the Australian coast.

We drove as far as we could along the beach, then clambered over the rocks of the headland to the next beach, which spread for uninhabited miles, backed by a tangle of yellow dunes and reedy grasses.

Away in the distance a solitary figure showed, a fisher-man standing up to his shins in the sea. Apart from him the beach was ours, from our feet to the far lilac promontory to the southward. We might have been the only other inhabitants of the whole continent.

After all, I thought vaguely, this is my country. And where in crowded Europe would we find this glorious sense of isolation? Not loneliness, but freedom was conveyed by that single fisherman with the whole shore to himself.

We ran down the dunes, fell, and tumbled over and over in the warm sand, laughing like idiots.

I still hadn't managed to ask Mother the question about the past that was bothering me. It was long ago, nearly ten years, but I knew we would both be embarrassed.

However the opportunity came when Aunt Flora succumbed to a diet of cream buns and an almost complete lack of exercise, and died of a heart attack (such an end was statistically becoming more likely, my stepfather informed me).

The day of the funeral, which I had reluctantly attended, Mother and I were washing up in the kitchen after the family tea for Mother's relations. I turned to her, the dishmop in my hand, and asked boldly, "Where is Daddy's grave? I know where Uncle Fred and Aunt Flora are buried, but not my own father. You've never told me."

Mother dropped a cup. Picking up the broken pieces, she made a small cut on one finger. She sucked distractedly at the drop of blood, and said, "Well . . . you see . . . when he was drowned his body was never recovered."

"When he was *drowned*? I thought it was an accident – a car accident!"

"No – no, it was a *swimming* accident."

"Well!" I felt winded. Why had I never been told? "But Daddy was a good swimmer."

"Yes, but that weekend he went to the south coast, the open ocean. There are dangerous currents in the surf."

75

"Oh." I was glad it was not at Couriyonga Beach.

"I'd better get a bandage for this finger." And she hurried away.

I didn't pursue the subject any further. She obviously didn't like speaking about it, and she was, of course, very upset over Aunt Flora. It was embarrassing, but I hadn't been able to shed a tear. Remembering how she had enjoyed funerals, I couldn't help thinking irreverently how Aunt Flora would have liked to be a spectator at her own.

Nine

On my boring round I had turned up one piece of interesting news, at the university, where the Registrar used to greet my arrival in his office with a little chant, "No news today, no news today," and repeat his time-worn joke, "The *Standard* has no facts, *Fact* has no standards," *Fact* being a local scandal-sheet in which the *Standard* had an interest.

Mr Ardmore told me the University Geology Department was organising an expedition to Central Australia, somewhere south of Alice Springs, to investigate a meteoric crater.

As geology had been my pet subject at school I now had a bright idea: if I enrolled for Geology I this year the university might let me go on the expedition and report it for the paper. It might be away for some time, as there was some hope that a piece of meteorite would be found and brought back for the geology museum.

The university year had not started yet, though it was rather late to enrol. Still, it was worth a try. Cadets were supposed to be given time off for lectures, and were even entitled to have their fees paid.

I took the AJA Rules book to Mr Parfitt's office and confronted him with the clause about university courses for cadets. He looked staggered, and took the book from me as gingerly as if it had been a scorpion. But Howard Miller, who sat behind me in the Reporters' Room, assured me I was well within my rights.

"And I'd like to do Eng. Lit. as well," I added brightly.

Mr Parfitt had boggled, but said he would see.

Now he sent for me and asked, "Finished that article yet, Marigold? You've been typing away very busily there."

"Oh! Oh no, not quite." (I had actually been typing out a poem.)

"Because as soon as you've finished that you might as well go home. There's nothing else on the books for you."

Encouraged by the thought of most of the afternoon free, I dashed off the article in fifteen minutes, and set off for home with the new, wet-ink-smelling paper folded beside me on the seat.

For once I would be home before Celia was back from school. If only Mother was out, I'd have a chance of exploring the cellar without being subjected to an interrogation on my motives.

But as I was going in the front door, I was stopped in my tracks. A loud babble of female voices came from the front room, Mother's friend Laurel several decibels above the rest. I was sneaking carefully through the hall, for it was filled with a large and precarious arrangement of vine-leaves and cotoneaster berries, when Mother popped out and said I could help her put out the oyster patties.

"But go in first and say hello to the girls, dear."

Girls! I shook my head and made frantic shushing motions. "Gosh, I could hear your friend Laurel right out at the gate," I said in the kitchen. I set the warmed patties out on silver dishes. Ignoring the suggestion that I might like to carry them in, I grabbed two sandwiches and a cream puff and retired to my room.

Even through the closed door I could hear the babble as the bridge game finished and afternoon tea began. I was beginning to hate women *en masse*; it was an occupational neurosis. Women's organisations and clubs, women making speeches, women wearing stupid hats I was sent to describe, women travellers coming back from all the wonders of the world and saying, "Australia's good enough for me."

I had committed my great, ineradicable mistake in the first place in being born a girl, and I wasn't going to be allowed to forget it. The National Council of Women, the Country Women's Association, the WCTU, the YWCA, all knew my face at their meetings.

No one except perhaps the resident Governor's lady could be as bored with them all as I was. I often felt sorry for the exiled Englishwoman with her tired, distinguished face. How she must long for the quiet of her county and the company of silent, masculine dogs and horses!

I finished the cream puff and listened to see if afternoon tea was over. A quiet had fallen, broken by murmurs of "Pass" . . . "Spades" . . . "Two No Trumps". Unless my mother was "dummy", I could sneak down the cellar now and have a look round without her knowing.

I was sure by now that something had been hidden from me over my father's death. Why had he gone swimming all alone? Or was there someone – another woman? – with him, perhaps? I wondered if there was anyone in Central Australia who had known him well, perhaps a mate with whom he had made one of those inland trips from which he used to return looking so brown and fit and happy.

As manager of a firm of stock and station agents, he had made this an excuse for the trips to stations run by big pastoral companies. Had he really gone to get away from my mother?

Once he had brought me back a piece of rock opal from Coober Pedy, and once a bull-roarer which I twirled round my head with a piece of string to make weird aboriginal noises.

Perhaps there was something among the old papers in the cellar that might give me a clue to those days. Nowadays the cellar was used only in a heatwave, when the icebox was full to bursting.

It was a small square room with a musty, earthy smell, led down to by narrow, curving stone steps. Apart from one meat-safe and a shelf of preserved fruits, it was filled with junk my mother had collected in twenty years of never throwing anything away.

A sliding-catch held the wooden gate closed. I juggled it open and turned on the rickety light switch. This had been temporarily mended years ago by my stepfather with an empty pillbox; for though generous over large sums, he hated small expenditures. He hounded down any of the family who left a light burning.

I stood a moment looking down at the yellow light falling on the grey stone steps where they turned. The cool, musty smell came up to me, and at once I was taken back into the past.

When I was little, before the ice-man came, the cellar was used every summer for setting jellies, storing butter and wine, keeping vegetables. I was always being sent down for something by Ruby, who had big feet and was terrified of falling on the narrow steps. When it was very hot upstairs I would sit on the bottom step to play with my dolls.

Now once again I went down and sat on the bottom step. The small window below the outside skylight was dim with dust and spiderwebs, but the room was not damp. Straw covers from wine bottles lay in one corner, left from my father's day, for Mr Hackett was dyspeptic and could not drink wine.

There were stacks of framed photographs and discarded wall pictures, and years and years of household bills pierced with spikes or held with spring clips, and an old calendar printed by my father's firm.

Tomorrow I meant to search the office files for a report of the accident in which he had been drowned.

We had never kept up the anniversary and I wasn't even sure of the month. I couldn't check the date by his tombstone because there wasn't one.

I busied myself with a pile of old school magazines. I had been in the third form when Daddy died, and it was just before the end of first term, nine years ago. That would give me the date near enough.

Now I inhaled deeply, and seemed to be drinking from a bowl brimming with memories. Down here I could remember my father most clearly, could almost see the separate bristles of his grey moustache, as in the detail of a Van Eyck painting. I could see his tall, broad figure – but perhaps he had not been as big as I remembered, for after all I was much smaller then. He had been given to bursts of boisterous humour, and equally sudden squalls of bad temper.

On Sundays we sometimes went for a family picnic with all of mother's relatives, but he didn't seem to enjoy these much although he liked the open air. He used to refer to the tribe of uncles and aunts as "your mother's relations", and said "God gave us relatives but thank heaven for our friends," and "Blood is thicker than water, they say, but I know which I'd rather drink when I'm thirsty."

He would make sardonic remarks about the elaborate food, and usually go off for a walk by himself while the younger uncles wrestled on the beach or threw stones in a mountain pool.

"A bit of damper cooked in the ashes and a billy of tea," he would growl, "and perhaps a dash of honey or jam if you want to be flash; or a hunk of corned beef cut with your pocket knife. That tastes better than all your cold chickens and salads and apple pies and things. Knives and forks! What next! And a tablecloth! You might as well eat

81

at home in comfort, without any ants and flies in your tea, if you're going to all this bother."

He said that when you travelled in the Outback you needed nothing but tea and sugar and flour, corned beef and onions; though people were getting soft these days and sometimes took potatoes and tomatoes as well, to go with the bit o' beef or hunk of mutton you could usually get at the stations to cook in the camp oven. And you came back all the healthier after a few weeks in the desert.

He used to tell me of the Afghan camel drivers round Marree, the groves of date-palms they had planted at Hergott Springs, of Oodnadatta and the Alice and Sturt's Stony Desert, and the plains scarlet with Desert Pea.

"Couldn't we go and live in the Outback, Daddy?" I asked him once when he came back, bronzed and cheerful. "Why couldn't we all go and live there?"

"We just couldn't, little one. It's a wonderful place, but it wouldn't do for your mother. She's a city girl through and through; even wants a chair to sit on when she goes for a picnic. She'd be no good in a camp whatever, and she'd be miserable away from the telephone and her Bridge Club and Aunt Flora."

"Then couldn't just you and me go?" I said, feeling a bit of a traitor to Mother. "I'd like to live in the Never-Ever."

"The Never-Never, would you? I wonder. Anyway, little girls need their mothers."

Then he had put me off his knee and lit his pipe, and sat there puffing and thinking, a deep crease between his brows.

"There's gold up there, you know," he'd said at last. "I know a chap up there who thought he knew where Lasseter's Lost Reef was. One day, when I haven't got a family to support, and you're grown up and married, I might go fossicking with him."

"I'm never going to get married," I said. "I'm going to be a man when I grow up and go fossitting too."

"I'm afraid not, pet. I'm afraid you got born wrong to be a prospector."

And how right he was! I thought. The sound of Mother's footsteps in the kitchen above recalled me. I went quietly up the steps and closed the wooden gate.

That night after dinner there came a yell of rage from my stepfather.

"What's this cellar light doing on? Who's been down the cellar? I suppose it's been on for weeks."

"Oh, sorry, Dad. I went down there this afternoon."

"Well why didn't you turn the light off? Burning away there!"

"What did you go down the cellar for, dear?" asked Mother.

"Oh – I was just looking in the tin trunk for some scraps of material. I thought I might make a patchwork quilt for my bed, they're coming in again now."

Mother smiled. She knew how I hated sewing, and that the quilt would never get past the thinking stage.

Ten

In the office "morgue" or library were kept filing cabinets full of cuttings and photographs under different heads, and a stand full of bound copies of the *Standard*. The current year was kept on top of the stand, marked "Not in any circumstances to be cut or defaced". The papers were nevertheless marked here and there with a gap like a missing tooth where an item had been razored out.

I found the files in the stand did not go back far enough, so I approached the cold-eyed girl in charge. She seemed to have been affected by the musty atmosphere of the place so that she was no longer quite human.

Asking for the right year, I lifted the heavy volume on to the reading-stand, and turned over the papers, looking at the front pages only. April, May . . . Black headings slipped under my fingers, photographs of footballers and beach girls, the Town Hall clock being cleaned, Julia the elephant at the Zoo having an oil bath, a pile of autumn leaves burning . . .

Another page fell back. I gripped the edge of the stand to keep myself from falling. There was my father's name looking out at me, beneath a picture of a distant southern beach known for its dangerous surf.

SUICIDE NOTE IN CAR

shouted the heading. I read the smaller type.

The blood sang in my ears, the walls began to sway and lurch. I waited for the ceiling to fall and crush me. A hot flush spread right through my body and receded, leaving me cold and trembling.

The file closed with a dull thump as I turned blindly away.

"Miss Trent!" the librarian called me crisply. "Bound files must always be returned to the shelves after use."

I turned back and lifted the heavy volume, clumsily, for my hands were numb. I walked out and round to the washroom and locked myself in the lavatory. A gritty grey dust decorated the window-sill which opened on a light-well. The floor was a dingy cement with an interesting pattern of cracks which I studied for some time.

So this was the mystery which had been kept from me for nine years! I had been driven by a restless curiosity to know the worst. Now I burned to know *why*.

I could still see the precise, impersonal lines of 12-point Minion type. My father must have thrown himself from the rocks into the sea, leaving his car parked above the lonely beach, with a note attached to the steering-wheel.

"Well-known city business man," it said. And "The police are satisfied there are no suspicious circumstances." The note had said he hoped his body would not be found, so as to spare his relatives the trouble and expense of a funeral. Two heavy lead weights, of the kind used on balance-weighing machines, with a length of rope attached, had been found in the boot, as though he had decided not to use them after all; or perhaps there had been more. The sea was too dangerous at that point for police skin-divers to venture in, but a search had been made of the beaches adjacent, without success. There were strong rips in the area.

What could it have been, I intensely wondered, that drove him to this desperate step? Financial worries? An incurable disease? Had he been "of unsound mind"? No, I couldn't believe it. It was a planned and deliberate act, a way out of some intolerable situation.

"Well, you can't sit here all day," I said, addressing myself briskly in the manner of Alice in Wonderland.

I got up from the closed lavatory seat and looked at my face in the speckled mirror in wonder. It seemed like a hundred years since this morning, yet it showed no change.

I could think of nothing but the tremendous fact which had taken the place of all my wonderings. Everyone had known the truth but me. Perhaps Mother knew why, but I knew I could never bring myself to discuss it with her. Ruby might have known, but I had no idea where she was now. Perhaps some clue did lie hidden among the dusty junk in the cellar.

Walking blunderingly back to the Reporters' Room I met Mr Smythe stepping briskly from the door of his den, which was smaller and more workmanlike than the Editor's stately room.

He looked at me keenly. "Oh, Marigold – I was going to ask you to come and see me. Come in and sit down a moment."

He sat on the corner of his desk and looked down at me over the top of his glasses with his gimlet eyes.

"Still keen on your job, my girl?"

"Oh – yes, Mr Smythe."

"H'm. You've seemed a bit absent-minded lately, as though you weren't quite with us."

"Have I?"

"Yes. And it won't do. We expected great things of you, you know. A journalist can't let his private life interfere with his job, he has to be single-minded if he's going to be any good. Now; is there something worrying you?"

I stared silently at the top of his desk. A lump was forming at the base of my throat, and my head grew tight and swollen.

"Because if there is, you can talk to me. I'm old enough to be your father."

I wanted to thank him, but I couldn't have uttered a word without breaking down. Surely Mr Smythe could see how my forehead was swelling, it felt as if it would burst.

He waited in silence a moment, while I listened to the loud ticking of my watch.

"Well," he said at last rather impatiently, "I can't help you if you won't talk, girl. You can go now."

I bolted back to the washroom and cried for ten minutes. Then I felt better. I looked round at the streaky walls, marked with lipstick and soap-stains, and wondered how many others had fled to this refuge before me.

When I stepped out of the office that evening it was raining, as if to match my mood. Yet I had no sooner roared up the hill in Strawberry than I felt once more that life was good. At the first intersection the ruddy-faced policeman gave me a cheery smile and a nod, though the traffic surged round him in a terrifying mass. Wheels hummed and sizzled on the wet bitumen.

I put my head far out of the side as I drove. The hills loomed ahead, softened by mist. Rain slanted past the headlights in golden spears. Life, life! I thought obscurely, flattening the accelerator on the wildly vibrating floor.

I took the longest way home, through the parklands where the grass was bleached and old, not yet green with the first autumn rains, and up to the foothills where I parked beside a silvery-dark grove of olives. The rain had stopped, though the sky was still clouded.

I looked at the unopened newspaper on the seat beside me, and thought of the news item I had read. There had been a picture of the sheer, terrible drop to the sea, the dark rocks over which it boiled and surged. I felt quite sick, remembering how on a beautiful day at Couriyonga, thirty miles nearer the city, I had stood on the cliffs, full of youth and high spirits, looking down at the rocks below.

I got out of the car and walked among the dark, twisted, ancient trunks of the biblical olive trees. It was dim and shadowed in the grove, though the sky was now clear. Somewhere a bell tolled out from school or convent, but to me it sounded like a passing-bell, the opening chimes of the Miserere in *Il Trovatore*:

Miserere! Again the wail of sorrow
For him whose eyes shall ne'er behold the morrow,
Miserere! A peaceful rest attend thee . . .

But to take his own life, even for the sake of peace! I was a disciple of life and a hater of death. I felt that I had to know *why*, and dedicated myself once more to my search.

One of the few places I still enjoyed visiting on my boring round was the Art Gallery; but now I felt shy even of Mr Muecke, who had known my father and must recall the peculiar circumstances of his death.

For a week after my discovery I rang up instead of calling in for news, and then when I plucked up courage to go and see him, he announced that he would probably soon be leaving.

"Yes, I'll leave this Little Athens of the South like a shot if I can get a good job interstate," he said. "The Board of Trustees have been hamstringing me for years. They want all the old story-pictures on the walls that they remember when they were children – and a long time ago that was! Space is so limited –"

"That's what Sub-Editors always say."

"–that I haven't room to hang the contemporary stuff, let alone buy a new Drysdale or an Arthur Boyd. Penleigh Boyd, yes, but then he's respectably dead."

There had been the usual letters to the Editor over the modern French paintings – the most stimulating loan exhibition we'd had for a long time – signed by "Mother of Four", "Art Lover", or "Outraged". One, to my amusement, had come from Dr Greeley: an intemperate attack on the moderns, and a demand for "a return to sanity" and the comprehensible beauties of the Impressionists.

Mr Muecke had read them more in sorrow than in anger.

"People like Dr Greeley," he remarked drily, "were the very ones who drove Sisley to a pauper's grave, and Van Gogh to suicide, and screamed that Monet had abolished form. Now they have caught up with the Impressionists and the Post-Impressionists, but are lagging far behind the newest movements. And in Australia, of course, they are further behind still.

"It's not the complete Philistines who shape Art Gallery policy, you know, those who know nothing whatever about Art. No, it's the ones who know a little and think they know a lot more, who 'know what they like'. Boards of Trustees are made up of such.

"Everyone who writes a letter to the paper on the subject believes he could run a better gallery than the Director does.

"Then there are the disgruntled local artists whose work is not hung. Oh, it's a hell of a job, believe me."

"Shouldn't the Board be made up of well-known artists?"

"I don't know if that would be any better. I think the Director should be given a free hand. The Board, now, wants to buy yet another Averil Brown travel poster for the Australian section, as if we didn't have enough already."

"I like his early work."

"Yes, but now it's just slick and commercial; the feeling has gone out of it, just as it did with Streeton when he became old and successful."

I pondered these double values on my way back to the

office. The best artists were often failures in their lifetime, the successful in a monetary sense were sometimes bad artists; yet some good artists were successful too . . . Was it just a matter of living long enough? How sad when they died or took their own lives, and all their fame was posthumous. "I thought of Chatterton, the marvellous boy, The sleepless soul that perished in his pride."

And I thought of my father, dead at forty-eight.

Lectures had begun at the university, which helped to distract me from brooding over his end. The Professor of English Literature was a small, neat man with spectacles, but he was a Writer and therefore to be revered. He strode up and down the dais like a restless but intelligent bat in his black gown, sometimes raising his head towards heaven as if for inspiration, or bowing it in modest appreciation of one of his own witticisms. In his drawling English he referred frequently to "the dreaming spiahs of Oxford", though it was said by the unkind that the nearest view he'd had of them was from the University of Leeds.

But his voice was preferable to our Lecturer's, for *he* was a new migrant with such a thick German accent that even his modern English was hard to understand, while his Middle English was quite incomprehensible. Chaucer with a German accent was hard to follow.

In Geology I, I found my old friend Dinah from school, for she had failed her first year and was doing it over again. We sat together in one of the high rows at the back of the geology theatre, and whispered and giggled through lectures, reverting to twelve year olds.

I sorted out my old boxes of rock specimens at home, and went about chanting "Cambrian Ordovician Silurian Devonian Permian Carboniferous Triassic Jurassic Cretaceous . . ." The Geology Professor was a real explorer who had crossed deserts of ice in Antarctica and deserts of sand in the Centre. We didn't whisper in his lectures, but hung upon his words.

"If ever I get married," I said to Dinah, "it will have to

be to an explorer, or a gipsy or something. I hate the idea of a little house in the suburbs."

"You'll come round to it, I expect," said Dinah.

"Like a queen ant!" I muttered.

"Like a what?"

"A flying-ant. When they mate, the queen bites off her wings so she can crawl into some dark hole and start laying her eggs. Think of it!"

Dinah said that girls weren't ants and you couldn't carry the analogy too far. But I wasn't convinced.

I was determined at least to travel first, and was still hoping to go to central Australia with the expedition to get the meteorite.

What a shame that my father had died so comparatively young, and hadn't been able to enjoy more of the open-air life in the bush that he loved! How he must have hated returning to the city, the office, and Mother's relations. But had he hated his bonds enough to make him kill himself? Once again I couldn't believe it.

For weeks it seemed that Mother and Celia were always most aggravatingly about on my mid-week afternoon off (for I worked all day Saturday), but at last I had the house to myself and made at once for the cellar.

I poked about the dusty shelves. Here was a box full of photographs and shiny postcards. I became absorbed in the postcards, forgetting what I was looking for. The strange arrested timelessness of those scenes of spring blossoms or snow-covered slopes, with small figures frozen forever in a gesture or a pose; the impossibly blue seas, the romantic precipices! I studied the crabbed and faded writing on the backs, but learnt little.

Next I picked up a large framed photograph, the glass missing. "Outdoor Meeting of the Australian Society for the Advancement of Science", I read underneath, and looked at the earnest young men, the women in light, long-skirted dresses, all posed in the thin shade of a gum tree.

There was my father, with what looked like dark hair and the soft unformed mouth of a young man, without his moustache; and there, surely, looking much younger, was my now white-haired Geology professor.

A pretty girl, slender and dark, with her hands clasped round her knees, sat next to my father on the grass. Was this some long-lost love? I looked – and looked again. Good grief! It was my mother. Slender, large-eyed, laughing, a lovely girl was hidden in the stout matron I knew.

What had gone wrong? Surely they deserved to be happy? But this was a fallacy, of course. "Call no man happy until he dies." I opened another box, and found old theatre programmes, invitations to openings of art shows, catalogues of pictures, newspaper cuttings; no letters or private papers.

When I had gone through all the boxes I stood thinking, chewing my lip. Faintly from above came the warble of a magpie as if heard down a chimney. There was nothing left, except the trunk full of cloth scraps and the bills.

I took down a sheaf of them held by a spring-clip which hung from a nail. They were accounts for groceries and hardware entered at a city store, going back for years and years. What on earth had they kept them for?

There were hundreds more documents impaled on iron spikes. Tradesmen's bills, house repairs, doctors' and dentists' accounts . . . Yes, here was one from the old doctor who had brought me through pneumonia and whooping cough when I was four. I could never forget his name – Dr Sweetapple. It always sounded like a name in a fairy story.

There was a bill for April, in the year of my father's death. "For Professional Services . . ." That told me nothing, except that he had consulted the doctor. Had Dr Sweetapple found signs of some incurable disease, perhaps? He could look up his records and tell me.

He must be retired by now, but I could trace him by the telephone book if he was still alive. I could see him now, with his round, merry, kindly face, and spectacles on a black silk cord; could hear his voice: "Say ninety-nine . . . deep breath . . . Again." His two fingers tapping the small cavity of my chest, the cold stethoscope pressing against my skin.

My father had held and soothed me through the terrifying paroxysms of coughing, and every night of my long convalescence had brought me some little present from town – a tiny white china doll with black hair, a wooden soldier, pink sugar mice with tails of cotton . . .

Only one thing remained unexamined, a large album of Views of Queensland in a violet cardboard cover lettered in gold. I opened it, and from between the pages of monochrome prints there fell a group photograph taken with a small camera, on one of my father's inland trips.

He wore a week's growth of beard and looked entirely contented, standing with one hand on the shoulder of a gaunt man with a drooping Henry Lawson moustache and a wide felt hat. He held a pan for washing gold.

I was going to put the picture back, but on second thoughts decided to keep it. I slipped it inside my dress, and went quietly up the stone steps, turned off the light and latched the gate behind me, just as Celia arrived noisily home from school.

Eleven

"Yes, I could look up my records of nine years ago," said Dr Sweetapple, taking off his pince-nez and polishing the glasses vigorously. He still wore them on the long black cord I remembered. "But it really isn't necessary. I remember your father's last visit very well, because he was a friend as well as a patient, and that was the last time I ever saw him. His body was never recovered from the surf.

"I was greatly shocked and surprised at his suicide. Since I started specialising in men's complaints, of course I haven't seen your mother. How is she?"

"Quite well. Married again, you know. But my father – I feel I have to know *why*."

"There is no doubt at all," he said, putting the glasses on again but looking over the top of them with kindly grey eyes, "that your father was in his right mind, as sane as you or I, if that's what is worrying you. And there was nothing physically wrong with him. He had asked for a complete check-up, and I was able to tell him that all his organs were sound, he had the blood-pressure of a twenty-year-old, and that barring accidents he should live another twenty years."

"Did he say why he wanted the check-up?"

"No-o. But he said an odd thing. I remembered it afterwards and thought I should have known what was in his mind: 'A man should have two lives, one to devote to his family and one to do what he likes with.' In other words, to throw it away."

"But why should he want to?"

"I don't know. He was a man who enjoyed life, he had great vitality. I thought at the time there must be some domestic reason; if so he didn't confide in me. I'm afraid I've not been much help, Marigold."

"Thank you, Dr Sweetapple, you have helped me. I've been imagining . . . You always were my favourite doctor."

"The first time we met you slid down under the bedclothes and refused to come out."

"And the second time I threw a book at you. But it was only a little book, a Beatrix Potter. Mother said you saved my life when I had whooping cough."

"Nothing of the sort! It was her nursing that pulled you through. She wouldn't let you go to hospital, but had a special nurse and an oxygen tent in the house. I told her, one night I said to her, 'She can't live till morning; it's double pneumonia, and there's nothing more I can do.' Your mother said, 'She's not going to die'. And by sheer obstinacy, I believe, she kept you alive through that night, and the next day the crisis had passed. She has great will-power."

"Yes, I know."

We shook hands and he showed me out. His consulting room was now at his home, and he insisted on picking some of his beautiful roses which he grew as a hobby.

At home, I sat in the car for some time, chewing on an old pencil and thinking.

When I took the roses inside and gave them to Mother,

she was quite touched, thinking I had bought them for her. I didn't disillusion her, but I rather wished that I had thought of it.

The university expedition was appealing for public funds, as when the meteorite they hoped to bring back was sectioned and polished, half of it would go to the Public Museum, put on display to show its interior crystal structure, and half to the University Science Museum.

Roma thought I had a good chance of being allowed to go, if I worked at it. I was writing a daily story to encourage subscriptions, which were being received at the *Standard* office, and a list of donations was published each week over my name.

"You have terrific energy, Mal,' said Roma. "I'd go if it was all arranged for me, but I wouldn't be bothered organising it. I guess I'm just lazy."

She had been going steady for some time with a young man who haunted the office in the late afternoons, and this worried me. Roma might get married and start having babies; she would turn into one of those boring young mothers absolutely dotty over their shapeless, dribbling offspring.

"Have you ever thought of suicide?" I asked abruptly. We were each eating a meat pie in her room, our feet propped on the desk among the spikes and sheaves of galley proofs, the wire baskets full of glossy prints and wads of copy-paper.

"Heavens, no. Think of the *effort* of doing away with yourself!

> "O! that this too too solid flesh would melt,
> Thaw and resolve itself into a dew . . ."

"Yes, but have you ever thought about it? I mean, I just can't imagine – to take your own life – when life is –"

"Oh, I don't know. Sometimes I think, if I had a choice,

96

if I could just melt away or drop like an apple falling from a tree, I'd just as soon be comfortably dead."

"Oh, no!" I cried, horrified at this negative attitude. "No, I believe life is good, however bad. It's better to be alive and suffer, than to be dead and feel nothing. We must live as if Here and Now are all we have."

"If that's all we have, it's hardly worth the effort involved, is it?"

"Stan, you're impossible! I bet they had to drag you out of the womb with a great pair of forceps. You'd want to float round in the *liquor amni* forever, lost in a foetal dream."

"You go out with too many Med. students," said Roma, wrapping the rest of her pie in its bag and dropping it into the wastepaper basket.

Mr Muecke was furious. So was I, because the *Recorder* had the story, handed to them on a plate by the Chairman of the Board of Trustees, Sir Murray Todd.

Dr Greeley had made a will in favour of the State Gallery, leaving it the whole of his estate and his collection. The catch was that the bequest carried conditions, and he wanted these carried out at once, not after his death.

He wanted a whole bay set aside for paintings of his choice, among them the Gallery's most famous picture, one of Monet's *Haystacks* series; a collection of Hilder watercolours, and all of the Gallery's Averil Browns.

"I just haven't space to hang all the Averil Browns, and anyway why put them alongside the Monet?"

"Dr Greeley has a Monet – rather a nice print – hanging behind his desk at the Hospital," I interrupted. "All gold reflections and pale blue water."

"The Board has been hamstringing me for years. Lot of old fuddy-duddies. Did you hear the comments when the French Loan Exhibition was opened? Incredible!"

"Yes, I heard them. I had to report them, remember?

Quote: 'These senseless concoctions of uncoordinated colour are apparently accepted as art on the other side of the world.'"

"Bah!" Mr Muecke flung himself back in his swivel chair with one of his wide gestures. He exuded energy, from his shiny pate and his rather protuberant eyes to his large, restless feet that kicked about under the desk as he talked.

"For some reason it is supposed, in this country, that having large amounts of money means having artistic taste in proportion. Take this Greeley now; granted his bequest is generous, and quite large for a private individual; but he wants to impose his old-fashioned taste on a whole State. It's ridiculous, and I won't do it. I'll resign first."

"Oh, please don't do that! You are the one bright spot in an otherwise dreary round. And they're sure to appoint someone Dr Greeley approves of in your place."

"I suppose we should be grateful he didn't ask for the Monet to be hung between *Favourites of the Emperor Honorius* and *Zenobia's Last Look on Palmyra*, or some of the other Victorian set-pieces that elder citizens used to be taken to see in their childhood."

"Me too! I used to love *Zenobia*, and *Under Fire!* and *Breaking the News*. You could get as much out of those pictures as from a full-length novel, with a little imagination."

"Literary painting!" snorted the Director, who was quite a good artist himself and son of a famous Australian landscapist. "There's a Board meeting next week, so you can expect some fireworks."

"Yes, and the Board will issue a statement in the *Recorder*'s time, the same afternoon."

"Well, I'll tell you what I'll do, I'll give you a statement the next morning. Either my reasons for retiring, or the reason the Monet will not be hung with the Averil Browns."

Twelve

Round the door of the Reporters' Room came a tall, gaunt person oddly dressed in shapeless moleskin trousers, an open-necked blue shirt, and a wide felt hat festooned with spider's web. A sad-looking moustache, tinged yellow with nicotine but otherwise of a grey colour, drooped on each side of his mouth.

This apparition from the bush marched straight up to my desk.

"Afternoon, Miss," he said. "You're the one runnin' this here meteryite appeal, they tell me? Here, I got some money for yz."

Five-pound notes began to flutter down on to my desk in a rain of paper. I thrust them back at my visitor, suggesting that donations should go straight to the university and were usually sent by cheque, "and then you can claim Income Tax deduction, you know –"

"Bugger all that," said the gaunt one amiably. "I wanter help this expedition to get this meteryite. You take it for them, Miss." He thrust the money back at me in a pile. "There's a hundred smackers there. I bin up North all me life, there's wonderful things in the back country. Me and me mate Bluey's got a gold mine up there, and she's a bonanza. I bin readin' your articles."

"Yes, well, we'll have to issue a receipt."

I took his name and handed him over to the Chief's secretary.

Back at my desk, I was greeted by much ribald mirth.

"Well, Danae!" said Malcolm Marchant, smiling with all his teeth. "A shower of fivers, eh?" I was in awe of him as he had actually had a book published.

"Marigold, I'm surprised at you!" said Howard Miller. "He's old enough to be your father."

I ignored them and began typing a note on the "generous donation by an outback identity".

Suddenly I stopped with my hands on the keys. Old enough to be my father . . . It was something to do with my father, something . . . It had been at the back of my mind ever since I saw the stranger's face.

Of course! He was the image of my father's old mate, the one in the photograph from the cellar which I now kept in my drawer. He could be the same man, allowing for the passage of time.

With a yell I leapt up and ran out of the room, along the corridor and down the stairs. He was nowhere to be seen. I went back and rang the railway station, checking passenger-lists without success. He had come from Bundoona in the Northern Territory he said, but his mine was somewhere out of the town. His name was Andy Wilson. I had a feeling he would never answer a letter. Somehow I must get out there myself and look for him.

The university expedition would not be able to set off before late autumn, because it would be too hot in the interior for travelling. At present it was too hot even on the coast.

A belated heatwave, the worst of the summer, had hit at the end of March. "Hit" was the word the *Standard* used, because this was a short word which would fit even in a single-column heading, and was one of the Sub-Editors' favourites. Weather "hit" the city, farmers were "hit" by drought, housewives by rising costs, as well as all the people who were actually hit by moving vehicles. It also meant criticise . . . that is, "Premier hits at strike threats –"

I had thought of turning in a sensational story headed "Meteor Hits Earth", and revealing only at the end that this strange and interesting event had occurred several millions of years ago; but decided it was not news, as small meteors were arriving all the time.

On the day when the temperature reached a record 117°F in the shade, the weather was a lead-story on Page One. I had to go to the Zoo with a photographer to report on the monkeys and polar bears eating ice-cream. The smelly cages full of listless animals made me wonder what they had ever done to be sentenced like this to life imprisonment.

In the *Standard* office fans whirred, boys carried jugs of water clinking with ice, and Freddie Flannagan's stock of chocolate frogs melted. Howard Miller fried an egg on the pavement outside, while a photographer took a picture of it. Even later in the afternoon, Strawberry's steering wheel was almost too hot to touch.

I had spent part of the day shopping, because the big stores had the most effective cooling systems in town. Cool draughts poured from their open doors into the scorching street as from the mouths of subterranean caves.

One of the pleasantest places in the city was the Art Gallery, with its marble floors and cool vaults, even though the air-conditioning on the ground floor had broken down.

I suspected that Mr Muecke might have thrown a spanner in the works of the air-conditioning plant, as this gave him an excuse for moving the more valuable paintings down to the vaults, where the temperature was more constant.

"It's too bad," he said with a merry glance at me, "that

the Monet has to stay downstairs for the present. But you know how it is in a heatwave – we can't get the air-conditioning mechanics to come, they're all busy."

This meant, of course, that he didn't have to hang the *Haystacks* in the Greeley Annexe with Dr Greeley's other selections. He had not resigned after all. He had merely indicated that he did not intend carrying out the Board's recommendations, and had quietly removed the Monet downstairs "for cleaning". It looked like staying there while the argument lasted.

By now the question of hanging the Monet had become a full-scale art row. Letters appeared in both the morning and the evening papers, for and against Dr Greeley, there were attacks on the Board of Trustees and on the Director, and demands for a Government inquiry.

All this was excellent for circulation from the newspapers' point of view, and attendances at the Art Gallery improved. Dr Greeley entered the fray in person, writing an intemperate letter criticising the Gallery's policy "under the present Director", which he said relegated all the best paintings to the basement, while "modern daubs and hideous non-paintings" took their place on the walls, such as bare-looking Drysdales, and ugly Albert Tuckers, which merely showed up the artist's inability to draw.

Mr Muecke read this one aloud to me, shaking like a jelly with laughter as he did so. "Why should he be able to draw?" he cried. "He's not a black-and-white illustrator. You know what Tom Roberts said, 'When you paint it's the colour that counts.'"

I said, "What are you going to do, are you going to resign?"

"Not me! I'm enjoying the fight. When that Monet goes up on the walls of the Greeley Annexe, surrounded by mediocre Averil Browns and little Hilders, then I'll resign. Meanwhile it's stopping where it is, in the basement."

Thirteen

"What happened to that pleasant young fellow – what was his name – Richardson?" asked my stepfather at the dinner table, which was about the only place I ever saw him.

"Noel Richards? But you hardly knew him, Dad."

"Didn't I? Nice, well-spoken young fellow. I don't think much of this boy with the noisy car. It's ruining my hydrangeas."

"Fancy! I didn't know hydrangeas were so sensitive to noise," said my mother.

"They're not! It's the dog who's sensitive, and every time that clatter-banging contraption calls at our house, he buries himself under the flowers and knocks half their heads off."

I promised to tie Bruno up in future whenever Sandy was coming. For some reason my parents always took a liking in retrospect to boys I no longer went out with. Perhaps it was just that one no longer in evidence was preferable to one in the flesh.

Noel and I had quarrelled on the subject of whether I ought to let him go to bed with me simply as a scientific experiment. He assured me that with his knowledge of physiology and general expertise it would be a most rewarding experience for me, and that I was missing a great deal. I said that if love didn't enter into it I wasn't interested.

He said love was a matter of chemistry and that I was a cold-hearted bitch who had led him on unfairly. So now we weren't speaking.

Whenever I went out with anyone at night I was subjected by my parents to a searching cross-examination, both before and after; but when I went for a drive with a man on a Sunday afternoon they were quite relaxed, seeming to have a naïve belief that the worst could not happen in daylight.

My stepfather would watch suspiciously while Strawberry had her fortnightly clean-out on the path by the back door – gazing at the growing heap of chocolate wrappings, newspaper cuttings, copy-paper, pencil stumps, broken combs, empty cool-drink bottles and rusty bobby-pins. Perhaps he was looking for evidence of hard liquor or contraceptives, but he never said anything except: "Clear all that mess off my path, young lady, and while you're about it wash your windscreen. It's a disgrace."

Tonight I was going to a party with Sandy, so I put on my best quilted velvet skirt and a gold-printed blouse. I snared Bruno with most false promises and put him on the chain.

For some reason my breathing became uneven, my heart raced and my face became flushed as I waited for the first shattering roar of Sandy's car. He was like his name, "long and lank and brown/As is the ribbed sea-sand", and he had me almost convinced that he loved me truly.

Sometimes, after several drinks, I even saw myself as the mother of a row of small brown boys with engaging grins and blue eyes like his, but with hair of a bleached streaky-blonde instead of dark. Then I would think of the ant-queen on her nuptial flight, and shudder.

The party we were going to was at the home of two migrant Polish artists who rented a house in what had once been a respectable suburb. The neighbours had already complained about the noise of the Sunday-night parties held once a month, which would overflow into kitchen, bedrooms, verandah and garden and go on till morning. I had been there before with Noel.

Noise at high decibels greeted us when we arrived, after a pause for parking, in which Sandy ruined my make-up. We'd had a hotel meal, dinner bolted down so that we could have wine with it before the bottle was whisked away at 7 p.m. Waiters hovered about ready to snatch the bottle, conscious of the members of the Vice Squad waiting outside, stopwatches in hand. There was so little actual vice in the city that they had nothing else to do but harass hotelkeepers and night-club owners with the outmoded licensing laws.

Even so we had managed to enjoy our meal; and I felt lit up and glowing like a Roman Candle as we pushed our way through the crowd to deposit our bottles on the communal table at the party.

"Pour yourself a drink," I told Sandy, who hadn't been before. "I can't see Stefan anywhere."

"That chap looks like an artist – the one in the wine-red coat, with the red lips and the Byronic curls," said Sandy.

"Actually he's a scientist, an astro-physicist, I think. The two who live here are Poles – they must have starved during the Depression, they're terribly thin-looking. There's one of them, sitting on the floor over there, with the beard . . . Hey, Stefan!"

He raised his glass to me, drank, and went on talking earnestly to a melancholy Latvian who painted four-dimensional pictures on long scrolls which could be unrolled and rolled up a little each day, so that the picture had extension in Time as well as Space. It had extension in depth because he used collage and thick impasto, which naturally tended to break and fall off with constant rolling and unrolling.

Stefan painted pure abstracts, patterns of colour like butterflies' wings, and his friend Stanislaus preferred semi-abstracts. They were both admired by Mr Muecke, I knew, but the Trustees refused to buy their work, though it decorated, in the form of murals, some of the city's public buildings.

"I haf first to win some big art-prize, then I become news, then they will accept me," Stefan would say with a shrug. The bearded gaunt-faced Pole was more like Sandy's idea of what an artist should look like than his small and desiccated friend.

"I suppose most of these chaps write or paint or something," said Sandy. "Who's that fellow there? He looks like an artist."

A wild-haired man in a blue velvet coat, his eyes wide and fixed, was gesticulating as he held forth to a group of rapt young women.

"No, that's the Bard. He'll recite some of his own poetry later on. He's a great asset at parties, except that sometimes it's hard to get him to stop."

"And that one with the grey hair who looks like a managing director, or perhaps a worldly Archbishop – I suppose you'll tell me he's a poet."

"Yes, you must have heard of him. He published that book of erotic verse which was banned in Queensland. The one next to him is an artist, or used to be. Now he publishes his own little journal and attacks everyone who ever did a critique of one of his shows. He *hates* art critics."

"Well, I hope they don't all get into a fight."

Around us the conversation rose and fell:

". . . and this jolly old bod from Pommyland is trying to flog a new edition of Flinders' *Voyage to Terra Australis*, when we've got our own per-fectly good facsimile edition at half the price."

106

". . . savage and destructive criticism. She is an evil influence on Australian art, an incubus, a –"

"And I tell you Man will destroy himself! 'For he who soweth the wind reapeth the whirlwind.' I see it in the rape of the countryside, the air contaminated with insecticides and exhaust fumes. I say –"

"–the unspeakable in pursuit of the undrinkable . . . God! Why did I come?" This was uttered in a low, bitter voice by the distinguished-looking poet as he made towards the door. He grabbed a half-full bottle of Scotch – perhaps his own contribution to the party – and disappeared.

We wandered through to the kitchen, and there, sitting in the sink – which fortunately had no water in it – was Noel Richards. His face lit up. He levered himself out of the sink – after carefully balancing his half-full glass of beer on the draining board – and embraced me. He seemed to have forgotten our quarrel.

"Marigold! Where have you been?" he cried.

"You know perfectly well where I've been all the time," I said, rather cross but returning his kiss from habit. "I thought we'd agreed not to see each other again."

"Oh, that,' he said airily. "That was a stupid idea. Forgive me?"

"I suppose so," I said, feeling happy.

"Who's this silly-looking bastard?" asked Sandy in an audible whisper. "Do you want me to knock him down?"

"Good heavens, no! Sandy, this is Noel Richards. Noel: Sandy Martin."

They shook hands without enthusiasm.

"I think I know your sister, Anna," said Sandy coldly, and went off to replenish our glasses.

"You'll never guess who's here!" said Noel.

"Well if I'll never guess you'd better tell me."

"Dr Greeley! The Med. Sup. himself. You'd think he'd keep away from gatherings of artists after the ass he's been making of himself in the paper. Someone must have brought him for a lark."

I looked around the big main room from the kitchen doorway, and located him in a dark corner, in earnest conversation with an elderly painter of gum trees who was equally out of place here.

"Do introduce me to him," I said to Noel on an impulse. "I just want to see his face when he is forced to acknowledge that I'm a human being with a name of my own like everyone else."

"Wait." Noel emptied his glass and dashed back to refill it.

We made our way to the corner. The two older men, standing with their backs against the wall as though they felt beleaguered, had reached the stage where each made long, solemn pronouncements, waited impatiently for the other to cease replying, then went on with his own argument without taking the slightest notice of the reply.

". . . the anatomy of the gum tree is a subtle and varied one, which it takes a whole lifetime of study to understand. Even now I am just beginning to get the hang of it. More like painting flesh than anything else – the contours of the limbs, the sheen of the trunk where the bark has fallen, the folds like the folds of the body. A white sapling, or a lemon-scented gum is like a woman. In my youth I liked painting women; now I prefer trees. You don't have to talk to 'em, and you don't have to make love to 'em."

"Do you suppose one of these young chaps could paint a tree?" said Dr Greeley. He waved his arm at some of Stefan's abstract swirls and segments where they leaned against the walls. "Not one of 'em can draw; just throw oil-paint and hope it'll stick somewhere and make a pattern, then call it something-or-other. I know what I call it! Better patterns to be seen under the microscope – groups of stained carcinoma cells – beautiful! But stuff like that is hung in the Gallery, while yours and Averil Brown's, half

108

of it, is down in the basement. Now they've even hidden the Monet away below somewhere. Scandalous!'

"No good painting gum trees these days, they say you're old-fashioned," said the elderly artist, and buried his lined, clean-shaven face in his mug of beer.

"Er – excuse me, sir," said Noel. "I'd like you to meet a friend of mine –"

"Eh? What? What are you doing here? Young Richards, isn't it?"

"Yes. You see it's a party, and I was invited. Marigold, this is Dr Greeley, Medical Superintendent of –"

"Eh?" He focused his small eyes on me, poking out his neck and looking more like a bilious snake than ever. Then he started back, spilling some wine on his vest. I realised that he'd been drinking a fair bit.

"No young women with red hair!" he cried, like a character from *The Magic Pudding*. "I gave 'splicit instructions they were not to be admitted. I have nothing to say!"

"I'm not –"

"I have nother to say, young woman, I don't care what –"

"Dr Greeley, my name is not 'young woman' and I can't help the colour of my hair, I was born with it. My name is Marigold Trent and I'm not trying to interview you. How do you do?"

"No better for your asking," he said nastily, and turned to Noel. "Richards, what do you think, do you approve of these ghastly modern paintings which pass as art today?"

"Well, I like the traditional *and* the modern stuff, sir," said Noel diplomatically. "But Marigold is more of an expert than I am."

"I like the French Impressionists," I said. "Like the Monet behind your desk – *Bridge at Argenteuil*, isn't it?"

He looked slightly stunned at my actually knowing the name of his print, but he did not reply.

Just then Sandy came back with our drinks. Dr Greeley turned his back and directed a long harangue at the elderly artist, ignoring us. I made a face at the back of his head and turned away.

Stanislaus, the small artist who was one of our hosts, had a reputation in Europe for his bitterly satiric cartoons. I noticed him later, with a provoking smile on his thin, sardonic face, look up at a large Scandinavian who swayed above him, clasping a half-full glass of Scotch-on-the-rocks in his great fist.

"Say dot again!" he suddenly roared at the Pole.

"Big dumb Swede. All you know is *Skol* and whisky and women –"

"Vy! You Polish scum! Say it vunce more and I knock your block off. I – I schlaughter you!"

"It is a great pity," said the other urbanely, "that so fine physical specimens do not have often the brain to match." His teeth gleamed in his haggard face.

"Argh!" Provoked beyond measure, the big man made a violent swipe at the artist, and found his wrist caught in a steely grip. Sandy's arms and hands were remarkably strong, and he had felt impelled to step in. He admired the little man's bravado, but he would never willingly, he told me afterwards, have picked a fight with anyone so large.

The Swede glared in surprise at his imprisoned wrist, then flung the glass in his left hand over his shoulder, and launched himself at Sandy with a roar. At the same instant Stanis thrust out a cat-quick foot and tripped him.

The thud of his fall followed a split second after the scream from a woman in a low-cut orange dress – a well-hated and influential art critic – who was standing behind, and had received the ice and whisky down her back.

"I think we'd better get out of here," said Sandy.

We stepped over the prostrate body of Erik, who seemed to have passed out peaceably with his head resting on his arm.

"*Skol!*" said Stanis, pouring some cold beer on his face to revive him. We fled.

We drove up to the hills to have a look at the city lights

110

and parked for a while in a disused quarry. I repaired my make-up on the way home for the sake of my mother's eagle eye (for she wouldn't put her light out until I got home). As we came gliding downhill to our gate with the engine switched off so as not to disturb the dog, I said apprehensively, "Whoever can that be?"

A car with dimmed headlights was waiting across the road.

The driver's side door crashed open and Noel Richards came weaving across to us.

"Hullo, Marigold," he said thickly. Then to Sandy, "She's my girl – was my girl first. You go 'way."

"Noel, old boy, did you drive here? You're not fit to drive, did you know that? Now you come with me and I'll deliver you back to the Hospital. Come on – hold up!"

Noel took a wild swing at Sandy, but Sandy's strong right arm held him in an iron grip. He was marched to Sandy's car and pushed inside.

"Goodnight, darling," said Sandy, kissing me. "I suppose he can come and pick up his car tomorrow when he's sober."

"Poor Noel! He'll have an awful hangover. Look, I'll drive his car and we'll leave it in the Hospital grounds, and then you can bring me back here."

We delivered him back to his rooms in the Hospital. "I see you know the way all right," said Sandy, retrospectively jealous.

As we emerged from the lift on the ground floor, I saw Dr Greeley returning. He was just about to enter the second lift. It was not a cold night, but he was wearing an overcoat, and seemed to be carrying something underneath it. When he saw me and Sandy he gave us one startled look, bolted into the lift and pushed the "up" button.

"Well, at least *he's* safely home," said Sandy. "He was knocking back the *vino rosso* at a good rate."

"Yes . . . But it didn't make him any more pleasant. I wonder why he looked so furtive?"

"Probably afraid you'd seen his dignity weaving along the corridor, somewhat the worse for drink."

Back at my place, because I was so late, Sandy coasted quietly to the gate. I hoped Mother might be asleep though her light was on as usual. The dog was tied in his kennel round the back. I opened the door stealthily, and without turning on the light, crept through the hall.

CRASH! There was a tinkle of broken crockery, the thud of the rickety hall table Mother had chosen on which to balance a massive floral arrangement including canes of bamboo.

"Curse it!" I muttered.

"Marigold! Is that you?"

No, a clumsy cat burglar, I wanted to say.

I spent the next ten minutes mopping up water and picking up broken china (for it had been a large vase) and then giving Mother a lengthy explanation of where I had been. Then I fell into bed and into deep sleep in the same instant.

Fourteen

A real, four-column head, Page One story had broken on my round, and in the *Standard*'s time.

Of course it had to happen some time by the law of averages, I had often told myself, but I was staggered all the same.

Someone had burgled the Art Gallery at last!

They had broken into the ground floor by way of the air-conditioning plant which was being repaired in the back wall; it opened inside and also out into the air where excess humidity drained away as water.

There was a great outcry: comments from Sir Murray Todd, the Chairman of the Board of Trustees; comments from the Director, and from members of the State Government hinting that questions would be asked of the Minister responsible about the lack of security measures.

For the thief, obviously knowledgeable, had not taken just any painting, but the Gallery's one French Impressionist and great treasure – the Monet *Haystacks*. Perhaps the recent controversy had given him the idea. Sir Murray was furious, but Mr Muecke did not seem as upset as he ought to be; and then I realised why; he didn't have to

113

resign now, because there was no question of the Monet being hung with the Averil Browns.

Also, he didn't think a real thief had taken it, but someone in sympathy with his own ideas about where it ought to be hung. It could even have been an art-student prank, he thought, in which case it would probably be returned safely.

STUDENT PRANK?

asked one of the cross-heads on my lead story. The sheer money value of the picture – estimated by the Director at about £100,000 – had impressed our Editor and appeared in the large headline. Underneath was a double-column block of a reproduction of the *Haystacks*, and the rest of the story nearly filled the front page. I was as happy as a cat in a creamery.

Then Mr Parfitt tried to take the story away from me.

"Better give any new angles you have to Jack Wilton," he said after the Editor's Conference next day. "He'll be handling it from now on –"

"Why?'

"Eh? Oh, he's the police roundsman, and they naturally let him have anything as soon as it comes in, and –"

"Why can't I handle it? It's my round. Why can't *I* get in touch with the police?"

"Well, Jack knows the ropes, and they know him, and er, well, you're a girl, you see, and they mightn't –"

"I don't see what in the world my being a girl has to do with it. I'll bet you when the picture's found, because Mr Muecke is convinced it will be, I'll get the story and not Jack Wilton. I'll bet you a hundred thousand pounds. Jack Wilton wouldn't know a Monet if it fell on him. He wouldn't know a Monet from a Manet, or a –"

"Now calm down, Marigold. You can write a piece every day, and if there's nothing new you can always do a piece about the Impressionists, and this Manet's life story . . . I suppose he's dead?"

"Monet. Yes, he's dead. Dead t'ree t'ousand year!"

"What?"

"Nothing. I'll get a comment on the security measures from Sir Murray, why was there no burglar-alarm in the vaults, why has nothing else been taken, and so on."

"Good girl. You keep in touch with Jack, then."

"He'd better keep in touch with me." I used to wonder what it meant when I read "She flounced out", but that is what I believe I did from Mr Parfitt's office.

Noel came round the following evening after tea without ringing me first. My stepfather called him "Neil", but was surprisingly affable. As I walked out to the gate with Noel, he said, "I was a bit full the other night, Marigold. Full as a boot, in fact. Just as well that bloke drove me home. I'm sorry I took a swing at him."

"You're lucky you weren't picked up for driving under the influence."

"Actually I knew what I was doing all right. But seeing you with that fellow really upset me. It was a good party, though."

"Yes. Dr Greeley had a few too many as well, I'd say."

"He left before me. But he must have had a terrible hangover. He wasn't at work this morning – had the day off. I wasn't feeling too good myself, for that matter."

Sandy and I had dallied for a while on the way home, so Noel must have had a long wait at my house. Dr Greeley had left earlier, yet he was only just arriving home when we came down from delivering Noel to his room. Perhaps he passed out?

Noel got into his car, then leaned out of the window and kissed me. "What do you see in that sawney Sandy Martin fellow?" he asked. "You'd be much better going out with me. Think how useful it is to know a doctor, for Ladies Worried re Health et cetera."

"I'm not worried," I said, "and my health is excellent. Goodbye, Noel."

He let in the clutch and sped away, after giving me a

look of what was meant for patient suffering. I leant on the gate for a while, thinking. The slow chirring of crickets made a background for my thoughts. My brain was ticking over steadily . . . *Chirr-chirr. Chirr . . . chirr.*

Suddenly it all fell into place. The stars, brilliant in the warm dark sky, glowed triumphantly. Of course! Why hadn't I thought of it before? I believed I knew where to find the Monet, and who had taken it.

The Southern Cross hung low above the hills, and westward marched Orion and the Dog. I gave a high wild cry and kicked up my heels like a brumby, then went racing up the path.

Fifteen

I was still writing a weekly story to encourage subscriptions for the meteorite-gathering expedition to Central Australia, but my heart was no longer in it. Even when I was invited by Dr Burford to join the party as a sort of unofficial publicity officer, my first thought was that I couldn't possibly go till the Mystery of the Missing Monet, as the Subs had immediately called it, had been solved.

MYSTERY OF ART THEFT DEEPENS

said the *Standard*'s front page on the third day:

Police have no clue as yet to the identity of the thief who removed the valuable painting, *Haystacks*, by Claude Monet, from the State Gallery on Sunday night or early Monday morning.

The painting, one of the Gallery's treasures, is valued at nearly £100,000. Access was gained by way of a faulty air-conditioning plant in the rear wall. The painting, which had been removed to the vaults for cleaning, was taken from its frame, which was found lying on the floor. No other losses have been discovered.

This suggests that the thief knew the Gallery, and knew exactly what he was after. Also he was probably wearing gloves, as the only fingerprints found on the frame were those of Gallery officials.

Police do not discount the theory that a gang of international art thieves may be operating, who will try to smuggle the painting out of the country and perhaps to sell it privately in America.

The Monet has been the subject of controversy ever since the announcement of the terms of the Greeley Bequest.

(Dr Greeley, Medical Superintendent of the Prince George Hospital, has willed his entire estate including a valuable collection of early prints and drawings, to the State Gallery on condition that works of his choosing are hung immediately in one bay, to be known as the Greeley Annexe. Among them is the missing Monet. Others are the well-known landscape studies of Sir Averil Brown, and the water-colours of J. J. Hilder.)

Dr Greeley, asked who he thought might have had an interest in removing the picture from the Gallery, supposing it was not the work of professional thieves, replied, "No comment".

He had, in fact, nearly snapped my head off and then banged the receiver down in my ear.

I felt more certain than ever that my hunch was right. I had asked him to waive his ban on "young women" and let me come and see him at the Hospital. When Jack Wilton tried later in the afternoon, he had no better luck. He was told that Dr Greeley was "out of town" and not available for comment.

I had a good idea where he might be.

At lunchtime I went round to Roma's room and found her eating a pasty, dropping crumbs of pastry among the glossy, socially-smiling prints on her desk.

"No wonder you have cockroaches in your files," I said.

"Listen, I've got something most exciting to tell you –"

"What are you having for lunch?"

"I'm too excited to eat. Come up to the roof where we won't be overheard."

"You mean walls really do have ears?" she asked, looking around the upper corners of her room with interest.

"Well, you never know, and I don't want that Jack Wilton to get wind of it; I think I'm on to the scoop of the century."

"But isn't he on our side? I thought you only scooped the opposition – that is, the *Recorder*."

"All men are the opposition as far as I'm concerned," I said darkly. "I have to show them that a girl can handle a news story as well as a man."

After she had heard me out, Roma agreed to accompany me that evening after work down to Booldinga, on the way to Couriyonga Beach. It was my idea that we should take two cars, to make sure of our getaway, as neither of the ones we owned was very reliable.

She said I ought to go straight to the police with my theory, but I knew what would happen then. They would either clamp down on the story and then release it in the *Recorder*'s time, or they would hand it to Jack Wilton.

Roma pretended to be bored with the whole thing; but it really was rather exciting as we drove down the South Road in the dusk, with all the lights glowing in garages and cafés – we stopped for grilled chicken and chips at one of them – and lighthouses beginning to wink along the horizon.

We drove soberly, occasionally passing each other on a hill, but not indulging in our usual clowning antics when we each had a car. Arrived at Booldinga, Roma parked at the end of the small street where Dr Greeley had his cottage.

"Do be careful, Marigold," she urged as I prepared to drive on to his gate. "He's a mad-looking bastard."

"I'm not scared of him," I said, shaking with fright. "Of course if he pulls a gun on me I'll just give in. If I'm not back in half an hour, go for help – you'll find the local

119

policeman lives behind the Police Station, and if he's not home get the Fire Brigade or the Surf Club or anyone."

"Then of course you might be quite wrong. And if he *hasn't* taken the painting you're going to look pretty silly."

"I'll just pretend I've come to interview him, because he won't let me be admitted to his office at the Hospital. He hates me so much already it won't make any difference."

As quietly as possible with Strawberry's straight-out exhaust, I drove along to Dr Greeley's gate. As I expected, his Mercedes was parked outside, and there was a light on in the cottage. I felt sure my hunch was right.

It all fitted together – his passion for the French Impressionists, his indignation with the Gallery Director, the disappearance of the Monet on the night of the party. Even without his odd behaviour later that night it might have occurred to me that while still under the influence of wine he had decided to take the law into his own hands and remove the Monet for "safe keeping". And once having removed it, he was stuck with it. It would be very embarrassing to have to return it when he was sober; and there was no question of putting it back in the Gallery, as, carefully shutting the stable door behind the departed horse, the Board had increased the alarms and devices to a point where it would be almost impossible to break in undetected.

I was sure he didn't mean to steal it; he wasn't that mad. But if the object was to stir up interest in the way the Gallery was run, and to show that security was lax, he had made his point. People who had never gone near the place except on a wet Sunday afternoon were writing indignant letters to the Editor. They owned a share of the missing Monet, and they suddenly realised its value.

The one thing Dr Greeley didn't want, of course, was to be found out. No doubt he would work out a way of returning it anonymously once the excitement had died down.

I crept up the path, hoping that Dr Greeley didn't keep a dog. Somehow he was not the type, I felt; more likely a Persian-cat man. The chintz curtains were drawn, but there was no blind. Putting my eye close to the crack between the curtains, I peered in.

He sat before the remains of a meal at a small table: a carafe of red wine, half empty, a wooden bowl with traces of a French salad, some cheese and crackers on a board, butter in a blue dish – there would have been a long French loaf if only one had been obtainable, I felt sure. He was pretending he was dining on the Left Bank in Paris.

One arm was thrown over the back of his chair and he was staring intently at the opposite wall, the back of his head to the window. I moved the position of my eye.

I saw the *Haystacks*, unframed, against the plain white wall, and it struck me far more strongly than when I had seen it hanging in the Gallery among many other paintings, or leaning against the wall in the vault in a poor light.

Leaning closer to the pane to get a better look, I bumped it with my forehead. Dr Greeley started and looked round. I stepped boldly on to the tiny verandah and knocked at the door.

There was dead silence within. I knocked again. Silence for half a minute. Then I heard steps in the hall, and the door opened about a foot. Dr Greeley stood there, looking his usual forbidding self, but less official without his white coat. His puffy eyes glared at me.

"Well, young woman? What do you want?"

"I want a word with you, Dr Greeley."

"How did you know I lived here? What is the meaning of this intrusion?"

Luckily I am fairly slim ("skinny", according to my mother) and I slipped through the part-open door.

"Shall we go into the other room, and I'll tell you?"

"No!" He barred the way, though the door between was shut.

121

"Why? Is there something there you don't want me to see? The missing Monet, for instance?"

"What on earth are you talking about?"

"It's no use denying it. I saw it through the window."

"Oh, you did, did you? Perhaps you'd like a closer look."

He opened the dividing door and I walked in. The doctor followed me. I tried to appear cool, but I wanted to bolt.

"There you are, young woman."

I went closer to the wall, and started back.

"But – but – it's a print!" I squeaked.

It was a good quality print, the same size as the original.

"Of course it's a print. You mean – you actually thought I had the original? That I had stolen –? You must be mad! And now perhaps you will allow me to finish my supper." He was actually smiling. I had made a fool of myself and he was enjoying my discomfort.

I slunk away, wordless for once, and joined Roma at the corner. Or rather I fell over her, crouched in the shadow of a bush.

She grabbed my arm, quite energetically for her.

"For heaven's sake, Mal! What happened? I thought he'd clobbered you and was bricking you up in the cellar."

"No . . . All's well," I said hollowly. "He doesn't have the painting. I made a mistake."

"You mean you let your imagination run away with you, as usual."

Roma was right; I had even written a story in advance, a lead story for the front page (I fondly hoped) telling how the painting had mysteriously turned up in the little coastal town of Booldinga, having been removed "for safe keeping" by an art lover who wished to remain anonymous and who delivered it to Dr Greeley's beach cottage. The doctor, a connoisseur of the Impressionists, had divulged its whereabouts to a reporter from the *Standard* who can verify, and so on.

I think I had imagined Dr Greeley begging me not to tell the police I had found him out, and promising to return the painting to the Gallery by a courier in the *Standard*'s time. I had been so sure I was right. I'd seen him coming home, late on the night of the theft, with *something* hidden under his coat. It only occurred to me now that it might have been a bottle he was bringing back from the party.

I'd left my story on my desk or in the drawer, I wasn't sure which. Though it was quite safe (for the cleaners had strict instructions not to throw away anything that was not actually on the floor) I was afraid, if I should be late in the morning, that someone might pick it up and take it down to the Subs. So we drove back to the city and parked in the lane by the side door which was always open.

We were halfway up the narrow stairs when the night-watchman put his head out of his cubbyhole to check on us.

"Oh, it's youse two – all right," he said, and popped his head back again. We were supposed to carry signed cards of identity, but he never asked for them.

The Reporters' Room was strangely silent and tidy, its floor of highly-polished brown linoleum free of balls of screwed-up paper, the telephone quiet, and every machine neatly covered on its desk – except mine, which I'd rushed off and left open to the dust and fluff stirred up by the cleaners. A light burned in the Chief's sanctum, but the room was empty; only the whine of electric floor-polishers from the far side of the building was to be heard.

The unnatural silence in a room usually vibrating with noise and activity was somehow intimidating. Roma and I spoke in lowered voices.

"I'm going for a Sweet Pea," she said, and disappeared. I found the article I had begun, and read it through regret-fully. What a story it would have been! When I'd finished I tore it carefully across, screwed it together and dropped it in the clean waste-basket by my desk. I went to find Roma.

Past the deserted Subs' Room, along the corridor and through the swing doors, I found a single eerie blue light burning in the huge dark composing room. The linotype machines, always so busy clicking and tapping out letters, were as still as giant insects arrested in menacing poses.

A dark shape slipped from the Stone and disappeared behind a machine. It was a rat. I shuddered and hurried through, feeling uneasy. The whole place, usually humming with activity, seemed to be under a spell. I half expected to find a cobweb woven across the washroom door.

There was no sign of Roma. Even the floor-polishers had stopped whining. I went into the lavatory and sat there thinking about my cancelled story.

Voices sounded from the outer room where tea was brewed – two of the cleaners had come in for a supper break. I had often seen them early in the evening but had never been here so late.

One of them said, clattering cups: "Miss Richardson an' Miss Trent come in tonight – I just saw her round in 'er room. What are they up to?"

"I dunno . . . Eh, 'ave you seen those dreadful pencils Miss Trent chews? They can't do her insides any good."

I ran some water loudly in case I should hear worse, and drying my hands, I opened the door and called brightly, "It's all right, Mrs Brinsley – my great-grandfather was a white ant."

There was a dead silence. Reflected in the mirror I saw Mrs Brinsley nod significantly at Mrs Bates, as if her worst fears had been confirmed, and touch one finger to her forehead.

I collected Roma from her room. We went down and drove to the pie-cart on the corner for a hot meat pie with tomato sauce and peas, and steaming coffee in thick white cups.

Everything else was shut. The wide, clean streets, bare and empty of vehicles, looked more lonely than a desert.

A few lighted windows showed where the nightly army of cleaners worked. Only the *Recorder* office was alive, preparing the morning's paper.

We parted at the edge of the parklands with a paean of toots which made a prowl-car inspect us closely. I drove sedately until they turned back to follow Roma, then put my foot down and went racketing through the night, by the light of Strawberry's rather cross-eyed headlamps and to the throaty music of her exhaust. Life, here I come!

The suburbs were thriftily dark, not even a street light still burning, as the Council turned them off at 1 a.m. As I turned the corner into our familiar street I switched the headlamps off as well. I went roaring through a black tunnel of roadside trees by a sense of direction only.

I couldn't see a thing. I could have killed myself, or worse, someone else; but it was one of those dares I used to devise for myself to prove I wasn't afraid.

Sixteen

The city seemed to have shrunk overnight. The temperature had dropped nearly 50°F. and I drove to work through cold, pouring rain. The heavy skies pressed low above the temporary-looking buildings, which appeared somehow small and mean. Yet in summer there was something attractive about their clean, light blocks under a blue sky, a Mediterranean air as of some city in Corinth or Tuscany.

But temporary. As if it remembered how short a time had passed since nothing moved on the gum-tree plain but kangaroos, and the wandering tribes of natives who hunted them with spears.

Autumn was coming; so the leaves were falling; so what? I thought rebelliously. At the end of the winter I had been expected to write a descriptive article on "Spring". Now I had to write one on "Autumn", to go with the inevitable picture of Council employees burning leaves in the parklands.

I could not think of a single opening sentence. What was new about autumn, for God's sake? Instead I composed a letter to Roma on the typewriter, letting the machine take charge. An extraordinary surrealist missive evolved, full of QWERT YUIOPS and HJKLNMS. I typed NOW IS THE TIME FOR ALL GOOD MEN, and ended in a burst of verse:

> And as from A to Z my fingers jog,
> The quick brown fox jumps over the lazy dog.

I sealed it in an envelope, marked it Miss Richardson: House, and gave it to one of the copy-boys to deliver.

The university informed me that the Geology expedition would be leaving in a couple of weeks. Of course I still wanted to go, but how could I leave with the Art Gallery mystery still unsolved? I nearly wore out the marble steps with visiting the Director's office; but Mr Muecke, though he remained his jolly self, could not help me with any clues. Nor did he seem overly worried about the missing treasure. He felt sure an art lover had taken it as distinct from a thief, though the police were watching ports and airports in case anyone should try to smuggle it out of the country.

"You mean someone who didn't think much of the Averil Browns? A sort of protest against the terms of the Greeley bequest? I thought Doc Greeley himself might have taken it," I said.

"No, why would he take it?"

"To embarrass you, make the point that you didn't value it properly, that it would be safer in the Greeley Annexe."

"And I wondered if *you* had put someone up to it – you were always complaining about the lack of news round here."

"*Me?*" I squeaked. And then I thought about it – what if I had persuaded Noel with promises of "yielding up my treasure", as they used to say in the old books? No, I didn't think Noel was desperate enough for my body to risk his medical career. Besides, I had a feeling I was saving myself up for Sandy Martin.

Then, a week later – it was half past ten in the morning, well in the *Standard*'s time – the phone on my desk rang.

Mr Muecke's voice said, "Marigold? Can you get round here right away?"

"Coming!" I said, and abandoning the Personals from the Melbourne Express, I grabbed some copy-paper and the new, unchewed pencil I'd just received from the Chief of Staff and sped down the stairs. Backing out impetuously I made a small scrape on the side of the cartoonist's car.

"Well?" I demanded as I was admitted to the Director's office.

"The Monet has been returned!"

"You've got it back! When? How? Who –"

"Hold on a minute. As to who, I still don't know. According to the janitor at the front desk, a young man came in just after opening time, and put down a long parcel wrapped in what seemed to be architect's drafting paper, addressed to me. He just asked for it to be delivered to the Director, and went. He was wearing a black beard, probably false, dark glasses, and a green felt hat –"

"Your man didn't detain him? Didn't ask any questions? Didn't call and tell you a mysterious parcel had been delivered?"

Mr Muecke shook his head. "No. Not one of our brightest staff members, I'm afraid."

"It's not damaged?"

"No. I had a quick look but I have to keep it for the police for finger-printing and so on."

"You mean you haven't told them yet?"

"Not yet. You begged me not to give the story to the police roundsman, remember?"

I could have kissed him. "And not in the *Recorder*'s time!" By this afternoon it would have been too late. And Board meetings, if he had waited for the Board to announce the recovery, were always held in the afternoon. "Oh, thank you, Mr Muecke. You are a brick," I said, beaming at him.

He smiled. "Well, you've always taken a close interest in the affair. Now, I'm going to suggest to the Board that the Monet should be hung among our valuable Australian Impressionists, the painters known as the Heidelburg School – Streeton, Roberts, McCubbin. That the Monet was obviously taken to make the point that it should not be hidden among mediocre Averil Browns. And that if it should be, they would have my resignation immediately. I think they'll see reason."

"Good. May I quote you?"

"No, better leave that part till after the Board meeting."

"May I interview the man at the front desk?"

"Yes, go ahead. But as I said, he's not very bright."

I thanked him again and dashed out, impatient to write my story before the police roundsman got wind of it.

MISSING MONET FOUND
Mystery Caller at Gallery

So ran the headlines that evening above the story I proudly initialled when the signing-copy came round. I didn't get a by-line – it was usually against the paper's principles – but everyone on the staff knew it was a Marigold Trent scoop. Mr Perceval sent me a little note of congratulations.

Even Howard Miller, my nearest neighbour in the Reporters' Room, was impressed; though he spoiled his congratulations by saying cynically, "It's all very well for you. Red curls and long legs are a great help when dealing with male officials."

"Only when they're human," I said, thinking of Dr Greeley and the Governor's secretary. "Some of them are monsters."

A stream of citizens visited the Art Gallery to see the Monet they hadn't even known existed before the theft. It was very good for attendance. Mr Muecke said they should have a theft more often.

Of course he didn't put it back in the vault when it was returned by the police. He hung it in a good light in the central bay, surrounded by burglar alarms and electric devices and several good Australian Impressionists of the late 1800s.

The Greeley Annexe was set up next door, with the Averil Browns and the Hilders and space for Dr Greeley's private collection to be added after his death.

No one was any the wiser about who had actually taken the Monet. The references became smaller and smaller and at last dwindled away. Sometimes I dallied with the idea that Mr Muecke himself might have taken it, or at least put a young friend up to it. He'd have known the painting was safe, and it was the sort of joke he would enjoy. Anyway I didn't want to know. It had been a good story.

Seventeen

At last I was to travel to the inland, where the original Australia was still the present reality, or more so than in the coastal cities. My blood beat high with expectation as I packed cotton jumpers and slacks, light sundresses and strong walking shoes for the heat, the burning sand of the Red Centre.

Our Geology lecturer, Dr Burford, used to tell us about expeditions across the desert, over endless rows of red sandhills so steep that the camels had to knee up one slope and slide down the other. We would not be crossing any deserts except in the comfort of the 'Ghan, the little narrow-gauge steam train which travelled the 800 miles north to the Alice.

The Chief made no difficulties about letting me go, for I was in his good books after the "Missing Monet" scoop. I was to send back a series of descriptive articles for the *Standard*, and it was hinted I might even be paid for them.

It was to be only a three-man expedition, consisting of the Reader in Geology, Mr Brill; a third-year student,

Brock; and myself, plus a workman we hoped to hire from one of the stations. A small truck travelled with us on the train.

I sat on the hard ground and fished one of the flies out of my enamel mug of tea made with condensed milk. Three more flies immediately fell in. The sun was setting, to my relief. Soon the flies would disappear with the heat. The nights were always cool.

The smooth trunks of the ghost gums growing in the creek bed – a sandy watercourse completely dry of water – had flushed a delicate pink. At noon they were as white as if washed with lime. The annual saltbush against the red ochreous earth, the skinny black hatchings of mulga and the rich curves of the ghost gums, all conspired to make me feel as if I'd stepped into a Namatjira landscape.

"Nature imitates Art," I murmured.

Mr Brill, a recent arrival from England, looked with distaste at both the flies and the red, dusty landscape.

His full name was the Honourable George Milton-Brill, but in Australia, and among irreverent university students, he had found it better to simplify this. ("He's the son of an Old Etonian Peer" – "You mean his old man learned to pee at Eton? What's so special about that?") He had large tombstone teeth and a flashing smile that somehow seemed false.

Brock, the third-year student, had told me on the 'Ghan that "he was not a bad old bastard when you got to know him". I suppose he was about forty-five, but he seemed old to us. I said I found his lectures rather dry and uninteresting, and besides he had a sarcastic tongue for late-comers.

"Yes, he can be a bastard all right, but he's not a *silly* bastard," said Brock, using the third nuance of that over-worked word in half a minute.

Mr Brill had decided that there was no need to put up the tent we had brought. Anxious not to be a nuisance, I agreed to sleep on one side of the canvas windbreak. Our camp was outside the crater rim, which was so drifted with sand and covered with growth that it looked like a natural feature until you climbed on the lip and saw that it was perfectly circular. It had been discovered from the air.

Some time in the geological past a huge meteor had crashed to earth, burning as it entered the atmosphere and melting and fusing the sand into glass with the intense heat of impact. Rocks had been twisted and altered, and the remains of the meteorite, presumably, were still buried in the earth within the crater.

We hoped to recruit a workman from the nearest station homestead to help with the digging. Mr Brill had not brought many tools, he intended to borrow them from the same source.

Already we had found a few small pallasites on the surface as remains of what must have been a considerable body of material. Even if it had disintegrated on impact, there must be some larger pieces in the ground.

We also collected tektites, the strange little "moon-buttons" of black stone, which were supposed to have been thrown off from the moon in a molten state and swept into the Earth's atmosphere.

As the sharp silver stars came out, swimming like fish in the green crystal bowl of sky, I walked once more to the edge of the crater and gazed with awe at its size.

The flat plain disappeared to northward in the dusk of evening, dotted with blue tent-hills. There was not a breath of wind, not a particle of moisture in the air. And the flies had gone to bed. No wonder my father had loved this country.

I took a deep, easeful breath and felt my spirit expand. There was something about the desert which was like the sea, or the top of a mountain – the purity of the air, the sense of freedom and space, the horizon's empty ring.

Somewhere out there, "on the far Barcoo, where they

eat Nardoo", was someone who might know why my father took his own life. As soon as the expedition finished, I meant to go on a search of my own for his old mate Andy.

In the morning we drove to the homestead along a dusty track that was sometimes only a cattle-pad, sometimes a series of "crab-holes" in a wash of loose pebbles.

Mr Brill drove the utility truck, and got stuck in the first creek crossing. He did not even get out but sat in the driving-seat directing me and Brock where to dig away the sand, to lay the wire-netting strips carried in the back, and to get behind and push.

After the netting had been rolled up and laid once again in front of the wheels, the utility was across. But my feet, on which I had foolishly worn open sandals, were burnt almost to the point of blistering by the sun-hot sand.

At the second crossing Mr Brill took it faster and we struggled through without getting bogged. After two more watercourses, both dry, we came to the homestead. Its surroundings were completely bare. Not even a clump of mulga had been left by the hungry cattle, the successive rabbit-plagues, and the droughts. Everything was eaten down to earth and stones.

But within the homestead enclosure was a small but luxuriant garden, watered with bore-water, where vines, fruit trees and palms flourished.

It was amazingly refreshing after so much red. If the cattlemen and their stock with their hard, destructive hoofs had created the desert without, they had also made the oasis.

We were welcomed hospitably if not effusively by the owner, who had had rather too many tourists visiting him uninvited in recent years, since the main road – such as it was – went through his property.

Morning tea was brought in by a part-Aboriginal girl in a clean print dress, with smooth, shining hair – I was told her name was Milly. Two tall sons wandered in, one long and lanky called Jim, the other almost plump compared to his brother, so he was known in the family as Podge.

Mr Brill, smiling coaxingly, wondered if we might borrow one of the station hands for a week or so, and "a few things" from the station store. Mr Grant the owner, agreed without marked enthusiasm. He was not a scientist and thought the whole business of carting a lump of rock back to the city rather foolish. If he had known we were then going to saw it in half he would have thought this sillier still.

He promised to give us enough beef to last us a week, and his friendly wife invited me to come in for a bath whenever I felt like it – bore-water only, of course.

We went outside to the cluster of buildings where were the meat-house and the store. I was rather surprised at the amount of stuff Mr Brill "borrowed" from the store, for which he didn't appear to be paying. He then borrowed a large crow-bar, and a man to wield it.

"Merv Darcey will go with you," said Grant. "He gets a pound a week and his keep," he added, looking hard at Mr Brill. "That all right with you?"

"Er, yes, quite, thank you," Mr Brill's smile flashed on a moment late.

"Good. I'll send him down to the gate. Well, so long." He turned on his heel.

Merv turned out to be a "battler", with a bony, broken nose, a short nuggety frame and humorous blue eyes set in a face as wrinkled and leathery as an old boot. He brought his own tools – a pick, a mattock and a shovel – and a canvas folding stretcher as well as his swag, which he swung into the back of the utility. He climbed in after it, seating himself among the bags of meat and flour.

"Last tram to Bondi!" he shouted as we took off in a cloud of dust.

We bogged in sand at the first creek crossing.

Merv was off the tray in a jiffy and working expertly round the wheels with his shovel. Brock and I got out but he waved me away. "Get back, it's not girls' work," he said.

When at last we lurched up the other bank, he suggested that he should take the wheel the rest of the way. "I know 'ow to take these bloody creeks," he said. "You gotta rush 'em."

Mr Brill demurred, but at last moved over. Brock got in the back. Merv, his brown calloused hands caressing the wheel, went flat-out along the dusty track, and without a second's hesitation, flew down into the next creek-bed.

The truck leapt from the bottom of the bank to about a quarter of the way across, hit once, bounded in the air, landed again, and took off like a kangaroo, coming down again on the far bank. Brock, who had twice risen in the air with all the gear in the back, managed to land again on the tray among the tools and bags and wire-netting.

"You certainly know how to take them," I said, letting go of the dashboard and flexing my white knuckles. Mr Brill seemed to be speechless with shock.

"Ar, y' get the knack of it. Drove on a mail-run, once, up in the Nor'-West. It was always sand when it wasn't mud. Drove a cab too, in Sydney."

"You sure your name isn't Mitchell?" I asked.

"Eh? No, it's Darcey. Merv to you."

"I was thinking of a yarn of Henry Lawson's."

"Good old 'Enery." And for the rest of the trip he entertained us with a recital of bush ballads by Lawson and others.

Good old Merv! It wouldn't have been much of a camp without him. It was he who stopped us sleeping in the soft sand of the watercourse, as he said a sudden storm in the ranges miles away could bring it down a banker and drown us all before we were properly awake.

He did all the cooking, much to my relief as the men had been inclined to look in my direction the first day, and I couldn't even boil an egg without burning it.

I would wake at dawn to the clatter of the camp-oven

lid and the bubble of steam as Merv attended to breakfast. Even if it was only boiled salt beef with onions and potatoes it tasted marvellous. He made damper and fried Johnny-cakes and cooked brownie pudding, all with only two utensils, the frying-pan and the camp-oven, besides the indispensable billy for making tea.

"Come an' get it!" he would yell each morning, and we would tumble out of our sleeping-bags, dash a bit of water on our faces from the 44 gallon drum standing in the shade, and fall to with ravenous appetites.

While working on my side of the windbreak at the fire, he kept his face studiously turned away from my direction until I was up – only a matter of rolling off the low canvas stretcher, as we all slept in our clothes. It happened to be Merv's stretcher.

After the first night of trying to fit my bony hips into hollows in the hard ground, I was stiff and bruised. Merv, the only one with a bed, insisted on giving it up to me.

He believed with old-fashioned chivalry that women were the weaker sex and ought to be cherished and protected. It was no use arguing – he even pretended that he preferred sleeping on the ground, which was obviously nonsense or he wouldn't have bothered with the stretcher in the first place.

"I'm tough, it don't worry me," he said. "I on'y have the stretcher in case of scorpions or death-adders walking into me bed-roll in the night. I don't reckon there's any round here, though."

I was certainly pleased to hear this.

As we all settled down for the night, the men on the other side of the canvas sheet, I heard him muttering, "A nice thing, if a death-adder or a scorpion was to crawl on her, lying on the ground. She'd just about scream 'er head orf."

I silently agreed.

A great white moon was shedding an enormous drench of light through the clear air. I lay looking up at it, thinking how long it seemed since I had seen it first, late at night, through Aunt Flora's window.

"O moon!" I began . . . My lids drooped. The rattle of the camp-oven woke me, and it was day.

On the third day we located a big block of meteorite, with the characteristic scalloped surface, dark and rusted-looking. It was firmly embedded in the sandy earth and would need a good deal of digging out.

Mr Brill estimated that if it was the usual nickel-iron mixture, it would weigh about half a ton. They would have to rig up a tripod with block-and-tackle to lift it on to the utility and take it in to the railway siding.

He was excited at the discovery. He beamed upon Brock, who had first come upon it. Mr Brill did not soil his hands digging himself, but directed the others where to dig. He was inclined to call Merv "My good man" when anything annoyed him, to establish the gulf between the leader and a casual labourer. Merv only grinned, amused. He certainly wouldn't have dreamed of saying "Sir", and in fact usually addressed Mr Brill as "You": "Eh, where do you want this put?" and "Eh, what about you – another cuppa tea?"

I sat in the thin shade of a ghost-gum and typed on my portable the story of the find. As I wrote, a fine sand drifted into the typewriter's works. Already it was beginning to sound gritty. A cloud of sticky flies tormented me, crawling into my eyes and mouth.

If I sat behind the windbreak to get away from the dust, the flies were unbearable, settling in a black cloud. It was better to be out in the wind.

I was beginning to tire of cold beef and boiled potatoes, when the boys came in from the station with some fresh home-grown tomatoes for us. They stopped for a mug of tea, but I couldn't face it in the heat of the day, stewed black in the billy and drunk boiling hot, either black or with condensed milk.

"Makes yer sweat," Merv explained. "Then it makes yer feel cooler." But it made me feel hotter.

When at last the sand had been scraped away from the sides of the meteorite, I took a photograph of it *in situ*, and then another with our leader standing triumphantly over its rounded mass, as though it were an egg he had just laid.

Eighteen

The sun rose in a thin white mist, pale and clear-edged as the moon, so dimmed that we could look straight at its ghostly disc. Mr Brill said it was not moisture but a very fine colloidal dust that floated in the motionless air.

Then the wind began, and the first eddies of sand and dust that heralded a sandstorm.

The sky darkened to a dusky red. The wind's breath turned fiery, scorching our skin and drying our lips. The drinking water in the drum was already warm.

As the wind rose, sharp sand and tiny pebbles came with it in a horizontal shower. Visibility was down to a few yards. We tried the cabin of the truck, but it was too hot to bear. In the lee of the canvas there was some shelter, but every fly for miles around had gathered there.

By midday the sun was an eerie blue plaque in a red sky. The air was so thick with dust that breathing became an effort, though we covered mouths and nostrils with cloth.

Somehow we endured until sunset. Then the wind died down and the air began to clear. Unwrapping scarves and handkerchiefs from our faces, we walked over to look at the worksite in the crater. The meteorite was nearly buried again in drift.

Just before dark, as we were sitting dejectedly about the camp washing some of the dust down our throats with tea, the Grant boys arrived to see how we'd survived the dust storm.

They looked at our powdery orange-red masks, the small clean area washed by tea around our lips, and grinned. Then Jim looked carefully at my bloodshot and swollen eyes, my dust-caked hair, and sobered at once. He had the same philosophy as Merv: girls were delicate creatures to be protected.

"This camp is no place for a girl," he announced.

Podge agreed.

"Haven't you even got a tent for her?" he asked accusingly of Mr Brill.

"Oh, er, haven't got round to putting it up yet, you know," he mumbled into his cup.

"Well, she's coming back to the station with us to have a bath and a good sleep," said Jim.

"Yair; Mum told us to bring her back," said Podge.

"And what's more she won't be coming back here till she's had a rest."

"Miss Trent will of course stay with the party," said Mr Brill.

"Who says?" asked Jim rudely. He couldn't help showing his antagonism to the man of science, whose English accent, which was perfectly natural for him, sounded affected to Jim's ears.

"*I* say she will stay. In fact she need not go with you at all. We are all suffering the same discomfort."

"Yes, but she's a girl."

All the men up here seemed to be infected with this old-fashioned protectiveness towards females. So far they hadn't consulted me.

"Miss Trent elected to come. There was no compulsion. Perhaps it is no place for a woman, but –"

"Then why didn't you put the tent up for her, you silly old blankard?"

Mr Brill drew himself up. His effort at registering wounded dignity went oddly with his dusty face and red-rimmed eyes. "I'll have you know I'm not used to being addressed in this fashion!"

"Good; then it's about time there was a change," said Jim, and then to me, "Get your things and come on."

I went meekly. The snag about being treated like something precious and delicate was that you had to let yourself be ordered about as if you had no mind of your own.

The homestead was a haven of comfort and kindness. I washed an inch of red mud down the plughole after I'd bathed and washed my hair, rinsing it with a jug of Mrs Grant's precious "rain". She seemed delighted to have me, as we pored over paper patterns and lengths of material she had been saving up till she felt like sewing.

But I knew I mustn't impose on them, and besides my quest was further north. And I was ill at ease with Mr Grant. He was a bluff bushman, expert at his own job, but with narrow ideas and a contempt for such abstractions as science and art.

"I must get some copy ready to send down with the station mailbag," I said next day, preparing to work on my creaking, sandy portable.

"You're welcome to stay here till you go south. We don't think much of these scientific chaps, you know, but you seem a sensible sort of girl. It's not that I mind giving this bloke stuff from our store, and lending him tools, and so on. But it riles you a bit the way he takes it all for granted. They ought to be able to finance their own parties, not have to bludge on the stations."

"They don't have to," I said. "This one was financed by public subscription, and shouldn't cost the university anything. I came to write the story for the *Standard*. I'd better go back to the camp and see how they're getting along, then I want to go further north."

He had come in while I was typing on the dining-room table, when I explained that I would have to catch the 'Ghan on its next trip north, to where I was going to visit a gold mine.

"Hey, Jim!" roared Mr Grant.

Jim wandered into the office with a large white cockatoo on his shoulder. It was quite free, its wings unclipped, but each day it flew up from the creekbed gum trees to see him and be fed. Its beautiful crest rose momentarily in a yellow-coloured ray, as I scratched its soft-scaly poll.

"Ay, you're going in to meet the 'Ghan on Wednesdee, Jim. She wants to catch it."

"Aw, we don't want to lose her yet."

I seemed to have become "she" or "her" with no name.

"I couldn't possibly wait for the next train, I'm afraid," I said.

In the morning I drove with Podge and Jim to the crater, to get the latest news and say goodbye to the men.

The sky was clear again, a soft, bleached blue in the heat. In the distance a line of low blue tent-hills danced and wavered in the mirage, floating above a non-existent lake. They broke into separate shapes, dancing above their reflections; then suddenly all ran together in a soundless collision, and disappeared.

As we approached the camp Jim gave a whistle of surprise.

"Well, you wouldn't read about it. He's put the tent up!"

"He must want you back," said Podge. "He's afraid of losing some publicity."

"You're not to stay, anyway," said Jim with authority. I was beginning to like being bossed by him.

Merv was putting on the billy for smoke-oh. The other two were out of sight beyond the crater's rim.

"When did he put the tent up, Merv?"

"As soon as you was gone. Moved into it himself, 'is

lordship did. He wanted me stretcher too, but I wasn't havin' any."

We walked over to the crater, where I took a photograph of the block-and-tackle they had rigged. Having lifted the stone, they would now have to winch it across to the truck.

Mr Brill ignored Jim and Podge, but told me they expected to have it ready to leave on the next down-train.

I thanked him sweetly for putting the tent up, but said I would not be needing it as I was leaving on the 'Ghan on Wednesday for further north.

"Half your luck," said Brock. "I'd like to see some more of this country. In fact I mean to come back next year in the May vacation."

"Come and stay with us," said Jim at once with automatic hospitality. "The old man doesn't like shooting roos – he's funny that way – but we'll show you some big mobs."

My opinion of Mr Grant went up immediately. It hadn't occurred to me that the mobs of giant red kangaroos we saw feeding at morning and evening were fearless and plentiful because, unlike most graziers who hated to see them competing with cattle for the feed, he liked to see them about the place.

After tea all round I parted rather stiffly with Mr Brill, had my hand wrung by Merv and my back slapped heartily by Brock, who had no illusions about the delicacy of girls.

As we had come in the four-wheel-drive buggy, the boys suggested they should take me for a short drive – only about ninety miles further east – into the range of low blue hills we had seen in the distance, floating in the mirage. They had a two-gallon tin of drinking water in the back, and a packed lunch of cold beef and tomato sandwiches.

I jumped at the idea of exploring off the track.

Soon we were in spinifex country, great clumps of prickly grass growing out of the firm salmon-red sand. At present it was seeding; the tall yellow fronds bowed down before our wheels as we jolted over clump after clump.

The hills began to lose their blueness after a while. We could make out their red, rugged scarps in which the shadowed clefts were deep cobalt. There seemed to be colour in the desert air, which put a deepening wash of intensity over pale grass, pink sand, orange rock and contrasting shade.

The hills, flat on top as a wall, rose up to bar our way. Jim turned the wheel and we drove along their base, crashing through an occasional stand of mulga. Then, like a gate in a fortress, an opening appeared on our left.

An ancient watercourse, flowing out on to the plain perhaps once in two or three years when it rained had cut a deep gorge through the vertical rock. The sides were as bare and almost as straight as in a railway-cutting.

Its bed was of coarse white sand, in which grew stately eucalyptus trees, their roots reaching to subterranean water below the burning surface. Heat-shimmer rose in our faces as we drove along the sandy bed, which was far smoother than the road we had left earlier.

Further in, the gorge opened out a little and there was room for pale yellow wattle and bright yellow boronia to grow on each side. We drove up on to one of the banks to boil our billy and eat our sandwiches.

After lunch we lay in the shade talking idly, staring up at the intense blue of the sky shut between the red and yellow walls. I had never known such peace. Far from "the busie humm of men" indeed! There was not even an unmade road for sixty miles. But there were the inevitable flies.

After drinking my tea I was still thirsty, so I drank a mug of warmish water from the tin, rinsed out the billy and virtuously washed up the mugs, pouring water over them as I had no dish.

Just as I finished this chore there came an outraged yell from Podge:

"Marigold! What are you doing with that water?"

"Just washing up."

"Ye gods! 'Just washing up', she says. Don't you realise that's the *only* water for a hundred miles? What if the radiator runs dry? What if we break down?"

"B-break down?" I began to feel alarmed.

"It *could* happen, you know," said Jim mildly. "We learn to be very sparing with water out here."

"Heavens, I'm sorry." I felt like a city-bred idiot.

After lunch we drove on a little further along the higher level, but the rock walls closed in again and we descended by a series of bumps to the smooth creekbed. As we did so, there was an ominous "click" from one of the back wheels. We went a little way in the sand with the momentum of our decent, then ploughed to a stop.

"Hell!" said Podge, who was driving.

"What's up?" asked Jim.

Podge leaned out and looked at the back wheels. "I dunno – could be the axle. I've only got front-wheel drive, and she won't go along in the sand."

We all got out and looked gloomily at the inert vehicle. I noticed suddenly how stupid and out of place it looked here, where a horse would never have bogged down. I suggested timidly that we might try and push.

"Push!" said Podge. "For five miles – in this sand? It would be all of that out of the gorge. No, it looks as if we might have to walk. Pity we didn't tell anyone which way we were headin'."

At this my legs became curiously weak, and I sat down on a hot stone in the creekbed. Sunlight beat up from the burning white sand . . . And I had tipped out half the water! The word "perish" rose in my mind and grinned at me like a gargoyle.

"There's one other way," said Jim, giving me a reassuring look. "The winch mounted in the back – we take the wire rope between the wheels to the front and hitch on to a tree and wind ourselves along."

"And when we come to the end of the rope?"

"Unwind it and find another tree. I think there are enough in the creekbed to get us out."

First Podge got underneath and examined the rear-end, but he couldn't find the trouble. "Probably in the universal joint or the sun-gears," he said, leaving me none the wiser. My mouth was dry with fright. I'd never walk a hundred miles in this dehydrating heat.

"Here, have a drink before we start," said Jim, looking at me. "A small one, mind – we'd better ration what there is, just in case."

They gave me the easy job – sitting inside holding the steering wheel and keeping the front wheels engaged. We made slow but steady progress towards the first tree, Jim and Podge coming behind to watch the rope didn't tangle, for if it broke we were in real trouble.

They took it in turns untying the heavy rope and hauling it to tree-trunk after tree-trunk. We stopped while they had a rest and a sip of water each. I refused when they offered me some. I knew they wouldn't be nearly so worried if they didn't have me with them, they'd probably been in worse situations before and if anyone came looking for us, the tracks would be easy to see in the sand. As long as they knew where to look in the first place . . .

It took us hours to reach the opening of the gorge. By then the sun was setting, lighting the orange-red cliffs in glory, but I could feel only relief at the ending of the day's heat.

The last tree was on the wrong side of the watercourse, halfway up the bank. From there, while Podge and I watched with hearts in mouths, Jim took the buggy in a flying dash down into the sand again. He seemed to touch only once, and with a tremendous bound and a shattering landing he was on the other side and up the bank.

Here the soil was gravelly, close in to the ranges, but we would have no hope of negotiating the spinifex sand-ridges with only front-wheel drive. Jim and Podge conferred. We each had a small drink of very warm water. I was almost past caring, with heat and thirst and weariness, for I had got out and taken a turn at walking behind along the creekbed, my shoes filling at every step with blistering-hot sand.

"Don't worry, Marigold," said Jim, pressing my hand and looking into my bloodshot eyes. I didn't even care about what a fright I must look. "We'll get you out of this, won't we, Podge?"

I heard afterwards that at the station, word had soon gone around that we were missing, as we should have been back well before sunset.

Mr Grant collected a couple of men, and with torches and hurricane-lanterns they set off for the worksite, hoping they might find us broken down somewhere on the way.

When Mr Brill told them we had left hours before, there was consternation. If it hadn't been dark it would have been fairly easy to see our tracks suddenly turning off towards the distant ranges. As it was they cast about for a long time until they cut our wheelmarks turning off to the right. The buggy had distinctive sand-grip tyres, and when they came upon fresh marks in the sand they recognised them at once. After that it was just a matter of following a well-defined track, except when they occasionally lost it in a hard claypan or patch of gravel. They had guessed we were making for the range of flat-topped hills, as there was no other feature on the limitless plain.

We sat about a small, bright fire of mulga, sharing one dry meat sandwich between us and washing it down with the last of the water.

We had retraced our route along the base of the hills

to where the sand-ridges began. Podge wanted to start walking, but Jim wouldn't let him.

"No; we stay together, and stay with the vehicle," he said. "If they don't find our tracks tonight, they'll get on the pedal wireless and have a light plane out to look for us in the morning. It's much easier to spot a broken-down buggy than a man walking. Besides, it's too dry a stage for walking. As soon as the sun came up in the morning you'd start getting dehydrated. We'd do better to go back to the gorge and dig a soak."

"Of course! I thought of that before, and then I thought it wouldn't do Marigold any harm to have a bit of a fright. It'll teach her not to use drinking water for washing up in future."

"That was a bit hard on her, Podge! She wasn't to know."

I thought it was a bit mean myself, especially as I had been privately resolving to die game, with a stiff (if dehydrated) upper lip. Now it seemed they had not been worried about the lack of water at all. We carried a shovel and they could dig in the dry creekbed till they came to the depth where water would seep into the hole, just as I had often done with my little wooden spade on the beach as a child.

We might get a bit hungry before they found us, but we weren't going to perish.

We were all back at the station by ten o'clock that night, weary but happy to be safe. The boys had been given a sharp-worded dressing-down by their father for taking a guest out to the ranges without saying where they were going, or taking extra water with them.

After a day's rest I had to be up at dawn, for the 'Ghan passed through the siding early. If we were not there to flag it down it probably wouldn't stop.

I said my goodbyes to the family the night before,

149

sensing Mr Grant's relief at getting rid of me before something else happened to put my life in danger.

Jim and I made toast in the deserted kitchen, and a big pot of tea. Then we went out into the cold, clear morning, where the brightest stars still showed in the paling sky.

We headed across the level plains for the railway line, a curling trail of red dust rising behind our wheels. Jim dashed through the creekbeds in style. We were in the utility; the four-wheel-drive buggy was waiting for some new sun-gears to come up from the south.

I began to feel sad at leaving Jim, as though he were a lifelong friend instead of a new one; yet I knew I'd forget him when I returned to the city. He was gentle in spite of his overbearing attitude towards me, with his pet birds and his slow drawl and his bleached straw-blond hair.

He stopped the car before we got to the siding, right in the middle of the dusty track. Several times we'd had to leave it to circle through the saltbush round a large bullock or a group of wild heifers with sharp, pointy horns.

"Marigold," said Jim. "Can I kiss you goodbye? I don't want all the train passengers looking on."

"Yes . . . If you want to, Jim."

"*Want* to!" He put out a long arm and I fell against his hard chest. "I've wanted to ever since we were stuck out there in the ranges. You were so brave and uncomplaining for a city girl –"

"Brave! I was scared stiff."

"You were a silly bugger all the same to have tipped that water out." And with this romantic pronouncement he pressed his lips so hard to mine that they were bruised.

Minutes later there came a loud honking and a truck passed on the edge of the track in a cloud of dust. We caught a glimpse of the grinning driver as he waved to us.

"Blast it!" said Jim, scowling. He started the engine as

a plume of smoke showed the 'Ghan almost on time for once. "The place is getting too damn' crowded."

The last I saw of him was his old felt hat waving from the side of the ute as he drove alongside the train. He followed it till stopped by a row of high red sandhills.

Nineteen

The slow, rocking progress of the 'Ghan – we had stopped while the engine-driver made a billy of tea for the guard and himself with the water from the boiler – delivered me to a small siding south of Alice Springs, where I was to descend. The mail-truck meeting the weekly train was waiting, and would take me to the little mining town where I hoped to find my father's old mate, Andy. The receipt for his hundred pound donation had given his address.

"Andy Wilson?" said the driver, banging the truck into the lowest gear and grinding over a rocky knoll and down into an eroded gully. "You'll probably find him at the pub. Usually comes in on mail day, though there's not much mail comes for him and Blue."

"Blue? Does he have a share in the gold mine?"

"That's right, yair, they're partners them two. Have been for donkey's years."

The truck began to judder over deep corrugations and pot holes. The sandy tracks around Yenta Station had been smooth highways compared to this. Conversation became impossible. I watched the driver's gnarled hands, the backs covered in sunspots, as he wrenched the wheel to avoid the worst washaways.

Yes, Andy had mentioned "my mate Blue" when he was in the city. I looked forward to telling Andy that the meteorite had been safely excavated, thanks partly to his generous donation. I felt that it was probably Blue who had the interest in phenomena like meteors; he might well be something of a geologist too. I looked forward to meeting him. The pale blue range ahead, which rose like a wave about to break across our route, contained the town which had sprung up fifteen years ago after gold was discovered.

At the pub, which announced its proximity with the increasing number of brown glass beer-bottles strewn by the roadside, there was a steady rumble of talk – male talk – from the bar. Tom, the driver, put my one travel bag on the verandah, while I, knowing that the bar was *verboten* to girls of any age, made my way to the "Ladies' Parlour" for a cold beer with a dash of lemonade. The first mouthful, to a gullet dry with dust, was always the best. The driver had gone into the bar, promising to look for Andy Wilson.

I was just finishing my beer when the Henry Lawson type I remembered appeared, still wearing the hat which seemed to be almost part of his head.

"Well, now," he said, shaking my hand. "Miss Marigold, isn't it, from the paper? We seen your article saying enough had been collected for the expydition."

"Yes, and we've got the core of the meteorite out of the ground, and loaded on a truck."

I hadn't sent my name with Tom and was surprised that Andy remembered it. But of course they'd given me a by-line with the meteorite articles because I was receiving contributions for the university. Usually they came by cheque; only Andy Wilson's had arrived in a shower of notes.

"Well now," he said again, "isn't that fine? Bluey will be pleased to hear that."

"I'd like to meet him. Is your mine far away?"

"Yairs; she's well out of town. And Blue doesn't come in much, he's what they call a re-cluse. But I reckon he'd like to see *you*." Andy was studying my face as if looking for some clue. "How do you happen to be away out here?"

"I came to see you. I wanted to ask you about my father, Harvey Trent."

He looked startled. "How did you know –?"

"Then you *did* know him? I was sure you did." I drew the photograph from the cellar out of a folder. "This is you, isn't it? I found it among my father's things, after he died. He used to speak about his mate up north who was a prospector."

"That's right." He looked down at the photograph, chewing his lip. "Harvey, eh? I never knew his real name. When he first come up here on his business trips, his hair was still red; so everyone called him Blue."

I felt an attack of giddiness. I swayed. I almost fell off my chair. It was, I told myself, merely coincidence; there were plenty of red-haired men called Blue knocking about the bush. "I – I came all this way to ask you if you could tell me why he took his own life."

He stared at me intently. "Yes, you've got the same red hair . . . I told him that."

"You *told* him?" I grabbed his arm. "Andy, what are you saying? That my father is still alive?"

"Here, take it easy. You look white as a sheet." He went to the bar-window counter and called for a brandy and soda. I gulped it, spilling some, for my hand was shaking.

"You must take me to him," I said.

"Well, now, I don't know about that. Blue doesn't like any strangers coming out to the mine –"

"I'm not a stranger! I'm the daughter he deserted when she was nine years old. He's supposed to be dead!"

"I know . . . Tell you what. I'll drive you out there, but you'll have to wait by the waterhole while I go and prepare him. He'll want to see you, I know. After he read those

154

articles with your name on, he was sure it was you. And when I come back, I told him what a fine-looking young lady you'd growed into."

Andy picked up some stores and a couple of bottles of scotch, some beer and a block of ice, and we set off in his battered utility truck, which had a large winch (worked from the car engine) on the back tray.

We must have driven ten or fifteen miles over a rough, winding and dusty track before we came to the waterhole, a beautiful pool deep among red-rock cliffs. Beside the calm water I sat and waited, my mind in a turmoil. Had he faked his own death, then? Or was he rescued from the sea with amnesia, couldn't remember he had a home and family, or even his own name? That seemed unlikely, since he evidently remembered it now.

I was tired and overwrought, and staring at the water I seemed to go into a sort of trance. I didn't hear anything. But suddenly I became aware of a man's figure reflected in the water, mysterious, upside-down. I looked up. There he stood on the bank, a tall grey-haired man with a beard and a tanned face, wearing crumpled khaki shorts and sandshoes. This was my father, and yet he was a stranger.

"Marigold!" he said, and stepped towards me, and I remembered his voice.

"Hullo," I said inadequately.

He put his hands on my shoulders and kissed my cheek. "Somehow I expected a – a little girl –"

"It's been nearly ten years."

"Yes . . . Do you remember how you used to call yourself 'Merridol' when you were little? And that's what you looked like: a merry little doll with red curls and big black eyes."

Yes, he was my father. I put out my hand and clasped his brown fist. The palm was calloused. My throat was dry; I couldn't speak.

"You must come back to the camp," he said. "It's fairly

comfortable there. I think I have a lot of explaining to do."

The "camp" was a surprise. They had built a substantial cottage of the local stone, which was a goldbearing haematite. There was no alluvial gold on the surface, so they'd had to sink a shaft, but the ore got richer as they went down. I was delighted to see that the outside walls, built of the first excavations, had some gleams and specks of gold in them.

The sun was getting low as we walked back, silhouetting the winch on top of the shaft and the heaps of new ore waiting to be crushed.

"It's pretty noisy when the stamper's working," said my father, talking to me as though I were a tourist. I told him I was studying geology and would like a look down the mine tomorrow: "The rock-face should be interesting."

We kept up the small talk during the evening meal. Andy cooked steak and eggs and onions, and I found that I was starving. We opened a bottle of scotch and some beer, and enjoyed its coldness "while the ice lasts", as Andy said. A bunk had been made up for me in the living-room. After tea he tactfully withdrew to his bedroom, leaving us to talk.

Yes, my father admitted, he had faked his suicide. He had found life in the suburbs, especially after returning from one of his trips to the outback, more and more intolerable. He knew that Mother would never consent to a divorce; the scandal would have killed her. And to desert her openly would be humiliating for her, and would condemn her to a single life. "Your mother is a home-maker, a born wife," he said. "But I wasn't the right man for a husband. How is she? Is she happy?"

"Yes. She married again when you were legally presumed dead. I don't get on with my stepfather, but he's not too bad. Celia's a little stinker, though."

"Celia?"

"My half-sister. Eleven years younger than me." I gave

a chuckle. "You know, I always thought she was a little bastard. And now it's true."

"Oh dear! If your mother only knew! You sure you won't feel a journalist's need to reveal the story for your paper?"

"Of course not! But if you realised how I've wondered, and worried, and brooded over this, ever since I found out about your 'suicide'. It was kept from me. I only found out recently, and it was a great shock."

I shed a few tears.

"It must have been. I'm sorry, little one. You were only a kid, I never thought –"

No, I couldn't condone what he had done, but I could understand as he told me his story of leaving the car near the rocks at that far southern beach, with the suicide note inside, and – final subtlety – the iron weights and piece of rope in the boot (as though he had brought more along than was necessary); as he warmed to the tale his lively dark eyes lighted up with the drama and excitement of outwitting everybody. He told me he'd hitched a ride back to the city.

Then he'd shaved off his moustache and gone to join his old mate, under an assumed name and a growth of red beard – for though his hair was already grey, his beard had not turned by then.

"I bet your Aunt Flora enjoyed all the gloomy details, anyway," he said. "Is she still on deck?"

"No. She died. Of overweight, I think."

"Poor old Flo." (She had hated to be called Flo.) "You know what gave me the idea for how I could disappear? It was when Uncle Fred was killed by the shark. If it had eaten him, no trace would ever have been found."

"But why suicide?"

"I wanted to make sure I would leave your mother free. If I just disappeared while swimming, she would have to wait for the law to presume me dead, and that could take seven years."

He poured me another glass of beer. I drank it, and suddenly yawned. I was deadly tired.

He stood up. "I'll let you get to bed."

He looked at me with a strained expression, solemn but with his natural good humour trying to break through. "Merridol . . . Am I forgiven?" He stretched out his arms.

I walked into them. "I suppose so," I muttered against his chest. He kissed the top of my head. I closed my eyes, feeling a surge of happiness. This was my dear Daddy, come back after all these years.

In the morning they took me down the shaft, and I saw in the torchlight the free gold gleaming in the rocks. My father gave me a small nugget which had been chipped from the rocks, and a sample of the haematite ore. I had to catch the returning train the next morning, so that night we went to bed early. Before going to sleep I heard a dingo howling outside.

Twenty

Sometimes after my return as I sat with my family at meals I longed to drop the news of my great discovery among their suburban complacency. It amused me to think I had a secret they would never know, any more than they knew about the little golden nugget I had hidden away among my underclothes in the bottom drawer.

I hadn't dropped even a hint to Roma or to Sandy; I'd promised my father not to breathe a word to anyone. Only Andy Wilson and I knew he was alive.

Mother had a family party to welcome me home, with all the aunts and uncles and cousins, including Uncle Fred's widow, who had dyed her grey curls lavender.

"And how did you like Central Australia, Marigold?" she asked. "A friend of mine was telling me it's not desert at all; a veritable paradise, she said it was."

"Yes, a paradise of heat, flies and dust. If it was such a paradise there'd be a lot more people, instead of less than one to the square mile. I don't notice everyone rushing out there to live from the cities."

I said this just to be perverse, because she always irritated me. A "veritable paradise", forsooth! Why couldn't she just say, "There's some beaut country out there, I believe." Actually I'd hated leaving it; not just the clear, dry atmosphere but the sheer emptiness.

I had promised to go back and see my father again. I couldn't feel quite the same about him, knowing he had deserted us; he had certainly been morally wrong to take such a tortuous way out of his responsibilities. Indeed it was probably a criminal offence to pretend suicide and deceive the police.

"Well, at least I left your mother a bit of money in the bank," he'd said in self-defence. "I only took enough for my fare up here, and to grubstake me and Andy for a month. It was a gamble, and we've been down to our last cent, but we're all right now. If ever you need anything you let me know through Andy, or write to Bluey Cole, care of Bundoona Post Office."

"I want to go overseas before I get too old. The nugget will pay for that, and I can sell my little car, though she's not worth much. Perhaps you were right to come up here and do what you wanted to do, before it was too late."

"The thing that worried me most was leaving you. I'd always hoped to get you back somehow if your mother died, but I didn't dare come near the city. It would mean gaol, I suppose, if they found out what I'd done; and your poor mother would be a bigamist."

He didn't seem really worried about it.

He asked after his pictures, and whether they had been sold. On the walls of the hut were hung several attractive designs in yellow, white and red, hatched with black. They had been painted by Aboriginal artists on sheets of bark.

"These will be valuable one day," he said. "When the art world discovers them, and how primitive and yet modern they are in feeling and design.

"I got some friends of mine to paint them for me, a long way north of here," he added. "They're natural-born artists, these people, with a wonderful feeling for design.

It's not surprising that Namatjira and the Arandas should be good."

"There's an Albert Namatjira in the Art Gallery now," I told him. He had followed the theft of the Monet and its repercussions in week-old papers sent up to him, where he had first seen my name in a by-line on the meteorite article, and felt sure it must be his daughter.

"I suppose you're eighteen now, nearly nineteen," he said. "And not engaged to be married yet?"

I shook my head. "I'm not going to get married for ages."

"Good for you! If young people only realised . . . As soon as there's a child or two, they're on a treadmill for life. I was a coward, if you like. I bolted."

"No; I think it must have taken courage to do what so many men only dream of doing. But you shouldn't have got married in the first place."

"Ah, that's easy to say! But you wait – it gets you in."

"I have been warned," I said, "by the Queen of the Flying-ants." He thought I was referring to a fairy story.

Yet why did my heart beat faster when I thought that soon I would be seeing Sandy again? I had dreamed of him quite often under the huge romantic moon of the Centre.

When on the last day I'd bumped away over the stony track, I felt I was losing again the father I'd just found. I rode with Andy in the old Ford – they were going to get a new car shortly, but he was attached to the "old girl".

I had turned to wave for the last time and blow a kiss. My father was standing on a heap of stones, his feet in boots this time, the sun shining on his grey beard, and one hand waving goodbye while the other brushed at the flies.

Sandy Martin, proving the adage that "absence makes the heart grow fonder", had taken to ringing me every evening after dinner. As soon as the phone rang I leapt to answer it, lifting the receiver with a trembling hand.

Sandy and I would talk for an hour if we didn't arrange to meet – goodness knows what we talked about, but there was a sweet communion in our disembodied voices. We wouldn't have stopped after an hour, but by then my step-father, goaded into action at last, would stamp into the hall and order me to "Get off that telephone!" as he wanted to use it himself, or someone might want to ring him.

Mother always asked, "What did Sandy want, dear?" as if it were possible to condense all those sweet nothings, even if I had wanted to, into something fit for a parent's ear.

"He's soppy," Celia would add, struggling with her homework in the dining-room. Then she would beg me to help her with her composition.

I had been home less than a week when the phone rang one night and I streaked into the hall to answer it, just beating Celia who had suddenly taken to answering it first.

"Hullo?" I said seductively, making a hideous face at Celia.

It was only Noel.

"Listen, Mal, I thought you'd be back by now, I read your articles in the *Standard* – jolly good. There's a party in one of the Residents' rooms at the Prince George on Saturday night. What about coming along?"

I wondered why I could feel no interest. Once I would never refuse an invitation to a party.

"Sorry, Noel. I'm still a bit tired. I just don't feel up to it yet. Still recovering from the Outback, I think."

"Off colour, eh? Well, what you need is some medical advice. You come along and I'll give you an examination, free." (I'll bet you will, I thought.) "Call for you at eight?"

"Noel, I'm sorry, but I really couldn't. Another time." How could I tell him I had grown years older in the last few weeks? Something was changed in me.

"All right, but I still think it would do you good."

"I'm just going to bed early these days. I feel as if I could sleep for a week."

"Well, another night, then." I could feel him hastily revolving other girls' phone numbers in his head. He wanted to hang up and try someone else.

"Yes, maybe. Goodbye, Noel."

I put down the receiver and wandered out on to the front verandah. The stars were much fainter here.

"Who was that, dear?" My mother's voice pursued me.

"Oh – Noel Richards. He asked me to a party on Saturday night." I couldn't be bothered explaining that I was not going; it would only mean more questions.

Helen, whose rather negative personality had been such a foil for Myfanwy, was leaving the office.

"Did you hear about her?" asked Myfanwy when I went into the Social room to see her on my return. She jerked her long cigarette holder towards Helen, who sat meekly typing out Social Notes, with her fair hair falling about her face.

"Going to get married, the fool." Myfanwy did not bother to lower her voice, but spoke in her usual gruff tones as if Helen were not there.

"Who's the lucky man?" I asked, turning to Helen whose usually pale cheeks showed a faint flush.

"That half-baked architect chap," Myfanwy answered sourly, "who's always hanging about the office. What does she want to get married for, an intelligent girl like that? I can't understand it."

"No, you wouldn't understand, Myfanwy," said Helen quietly. It was the first time I had ever heard her answer back.

The Social Editress snorted and jerked a pile of copy-paper towards her. She began writing furiously in her large, beautiful script. I smiled at Helen and left. There was no doubt she looked blooming; love agreed with her.

And Roma was leaving too. Running *away* from love, in her case. She was going to another State, where she was to join one of those glossy weekly magazines in which the

163

advertisements are more colourful and contain less facts than the fiction. We used to make plans for going to Europe together, for passages on German cargo boats to Antwerp were cheap. She would never go with me now.

My brief holiday had made me restless. I hated the office. I couldn't settle down to study, and spent a lot of time outside the windows of shipping companies, looking at those fascinating models of ships with all their little portholes and stanchions and lifeboats.

I would imagine myself leaning on the miniature rail and gazing over an endless expanse of blue – the Indian Ocean – while flying fish skipped away from the bow-wave in flashes of silver.

Twenty-One

My spirits always rose with the return of summer, just as
Orion rose once more in the east, the giant Saucepan my
father used to point out to me when I was a little girl and
we lay outside on the lawn to escape the heat of the house.

The Saucepan, symbol of housewifely arts – or a hero's
jewelled belt and sword! They were two views of the same
arrangement of stars, yet how different; I rejected the
utilitarian pot for the glitter of jewels, the loaf of bread for
the bunch of white hyacinths.

The choice came sooner than I expected.

Already in October the temperatures had reached the
nineties, and in November we had our first century for the
summer. The grassy hills were beginning to turn brown
and yellow as ripe wheat.

In the afternoon the sky at the zenith was dark-blue,
almost purple, with a few motionless white clouds casting
shadows on the plain.

I felt a longing for the sea, which was miles away from
the city. As soon as I was free I rang Sandy, who was
supposed to be studying, and arranged to pick him up.
Soon we were driving down the South Road in Strawberry,

with the hood down. The breeze of our movement made the heat seem less.

We climbed the first hill. The coloured landscape lay open before us: the paddocks grassed with gold and the band of sea deep blue against the sky.

> "Blue and gold, blue and gold,
> Glorious, glorious gold and blue,"

I sang to the muffled roar of Strawberry's straight-out exhaust.

My hair and my short skirt fluttered in the breeze, so Sandy thoughtfully held the skirt down for me while I was driving; but then his hand somehow got underneath it instead of on top.

I wasn't concentrating very well. After I had swerved over the centre line and nearly hit a bus coming the other way, he said, "For God's sake pull up and let me drive before you kill us both. You must have a hidden death wish, the way you drive."

"Well, I assure you I haven't," I said, pulling on to the dry grass verge. I moved over and nursed my right foot which was burning from being pressed on the red-hot accelerator pedal. We were both hatless, though the sun stood nearly overhead, reflected dazzlingly from the chrome and glass of passing cars. The car seats were almost smoking. "Quick, quick, get going before I melt!"

When we got to "our" beach, there were two or three family parties ahead of us. It could be reached only through a difficult wire gate and along an unmade track. Sandy scowled and muttered that the place was getting overrun with people, and I thought of Jim, with his pet cockatoo and his lazy drawl, six hundred miles away.

We ran quickly over the sandhills, for the sand burned our feet. And there lay the wide, cool sea. It was smooth as watered silk, green in the shallows and utterly clear, so that the sunbeams wavered brightly on the sand beneath.

166

Sandy swam out towards the blue line of deeper water, but I refused to go far out. Ever since the tragedy in our family I had been conditioned to a fear of sharks, and all the time I felt my eyes turning uneasily, looking for a dark shadow in the water. It was not enough to make me give up swimming, but it was ever-present, so that I could never quite relax and enjoy the water.

At last we came out and lay on our towels on the sand. The steady progression of waves towards the shore, small perfect waves in a still sea without ripples or cross-currents, lulled me almost to sleep.

Like as the waves make towards the pebbled shore . . .

Well, they might have pebbled shores in England, but I preferred the beautiful sweep of white sand sloping gently down to water so clean and pure that it looked good enough to drink.

When the sun set the family parties had all packed up and gone home. Sandy, who by now was living up to his name, with sand-crystals even in his eyebrows, peeled off my costume and carried me down to the sea and dunked me in the glowing waters. The sea gleamed with colour, green and amethyst and yellow, like one of Dr Greeley's favourite Impressionist paintings, brilliant as the *Bay at St Ives* by David Davies. I expect there is sand at St Ives, I thought. I'll have to go to Cornwall one day.

Just now I was very much here, at beautiful Maslin's beach in South Australia. And I had a feeling something very important was about to happen.

The air was already starting to cool. We ran up the beach to the dry sand, which still held the day's heat. Sandy dried the wet ends of my hair, and kissed the back of my neck, then laid me out flat on my spread towel. He knelt beside me and contemplated my leggy, naked figure from head to toe, then with a sort of groan he fell on me.

It was exciting all right, but truthfully not all I had

expected. Noel, who had been reading D. H. Lawrence, had warned me about "sex in the head" and my head was full of all sorts of wrong conceptions. However I had enjoyed the preliminaries. The setting was perfect, anyway. The stars were beginning to come out as the sky turned peacock and apricot. The Southern Cross hung low above the sea.

"I will remember this forever," I said.

Sandy stirred, and kissed me gently. "Of course, I want it to be forever, darling," he said soberly.

I sat up in alarm. "Sandy, we mustn't think of this as a beginning, but as a very perfect ending."

"What on earth are you talking about?" He slapped irritably at a mosquito. "I'm asking you to marry me, you dill."

"I mean I don't want a relationship that's for always. I hate the word 'forever'. I don't want to be tied down with children and wedding rings and till death us do part –"

"All *right*. You'll never be the mother of any child of mine. And I shan't ask you again." He began to dress.

It sounded very chill and final. I shivered. "Oh dear!" I said, "I didn't mean it to sound like that, and now you're hurt."

I kissed him humbly and wept a little, but we quarrelled again on the way home. So our day did not end perfectly after all.

Once, as the car climbed a rise, I could see in the distance all the lights of the city, twinkling like stars, white and green and amber and red and gold. I watched the telephone poles go stitching past, looping up the wires which gleamed in the headlights like threads of spun gold.

The President of the Housewives' Society was on her feet, making a speech about the price of tea. I didn't like tea and was not a housewife, so my mind was far away, though

168

I folded a wad of copy-paper on my knees and strove to look intelligent and attentive.

I took a good look round at the housewives, and their representatives on the platform. They were either over-weight and shapeless, or thin and dried-up and angular, with stringy necks and too-bright lipstick making their mouths look hard. The President looked as if she lived on over-stewed tea and sour pickles.

There was a sameness about the faces, thin or fat – what was it that they all had in common? Resignation, that was it. The down-turned mouth, the flaccid jaw, the droop at the outer corners of the eyes . . . And this was what marriage and motherhood had done for them!

I thought of my own mother, that lovely, slender, ethereal-looking girl in the old portrait in the cellar, smiling under an extinguishing hat. A middle-age spread had over-taken her, the bright eyes had faded, the dark hair was grey, and a deep, troubled frown was etched into the once smooth forehead.

I looked at the faces in the hall, fat and flabby or lined and sharp, and thought, Never! My eyes are open, and they'll never get me.

It didn't occur to me that what had caused the universal changes might be simply age rather than marriage; nearly all the older women I knew *were* married, and my logic seemed infallible.

I had my piece of gold stashed away in the bottom drawer of my dressing-table at home, and enough savings in the bank for my fare overseas. All I needed was to make the effort.

It was only leaving Sandy that would be difficult. But if I was in love with Sandy it was for the wrong reasons, and they were not enough to base a lifetime together on. The only way to tell if it was the real thing was to go away for a while.

I had to explain this very seriously to Sandy, for of course what happened on that sunset beach was a beginning and not an ending. The warm summer nights were my undoing, and all those stars.

On sunny Sundays we drove miles to get away from people. The hollowed sandhills above the beaches, the secluded gullies in the hills – we sought them out with one purpose, to be alone together; and at the same time discovered each other and a great many beautiful haunts.

There was one gully in the ranges with a small river flowing through it, with a name like a chime of little bells – Onkaparinga. (Why did we ever look beyond the native names, so musical and so apt?)

The water fell tinkling from rockpool to rockpool, then widened into a big shallow swimming-hole beneath a towering cliff. It was sheltered from every wind, bowered deep in gum-tree scrub and melaleuca:

> There is a river in the range
> I love to think about;
> Perhaps the searching feet of change
> Have never found it out . . .

I don't suppose it was Kendall's river, but it was beautiful enough to have inspired a poet. White saplings, all their bark peeled away as though they had dropped their clothes about their feet, stood round the water's edge in quiet contemplation of their own reflections. While we lay still, little wrens blue as butterflies, with several little round brown wives, came bobbing out of the scrub to inspect us.

We swam and sunbathed and made love under the blessing of the sun, then swam again and spread ourselves on the warm rocks to dry. We boiled the billy and ate sandwiches and made love again under the stars and above a great many hard rocks, which was all very well for Sandy. But in spite of the discomforts I liked it better all the time. I perceived that at this rate I would very soon be sunk. Even if I didn't go and have a baby, I would never be able to give him up. Against all my deepest feminine instincts, something warned me: this is not what you really want, and you'll be sorry.

I explained to Sandy that it would have to stop if I was to get things into perspective and be able to tell whether I really loved him enough to marry him. It was in his own interests, I explained cunningly. We would declare a truce in the battle of love, and lay down our arms.

It would obviously be very difficult for both of us to keep to the terms of the agreement. The best thing would be for me to go away for a while, right away, so that we could only communicate by letters.

"You mean you're going to the Centre again? On another expedition?"

"No. Overseas. On one of those little white liners in the shipping companies' windows . . ."

What finally set me off was a small thing in itself, a kind of last straw.

I arrived home to find my mother waiting in a state of suppressed excitement and curiosity.

"Marigold!" she cried. "Why didn't you tell us you had valuables hidden in your room! We might have been burgled! This *is* gold, isn't it?" She was holding my precious nugget.

"Who said you could take that out of my drawer!" I was furious.

"Celia found it. She was going to borrow that pink slip from you, she's getting so big and growing out of hers – "

"That's no reason to take mine. And I'm sick of Celia poking in my drawers, she's always doing it. I wish she'd keep out of my room!"

"But where did you *get* it, dear? Did you find it up in the Centre when you were on that university expedition? Why didn't you tell us?"

"Mother, what does it matter? Yes, I found it. There wasn't any more, it was just a lucky find, a piece of alluvial gold lying on the surface. I was keeping it for a rainy day."

"Well, you were foolish to keep it in the house. Why

didn't you put it in the bank? Or change it into money?"

"Because I like it. I take it out and look at it. I don't know why I didn't tell you, I suppose I wanted a secret of my own?"

"A secret!" said my mother rather bitterly. "Everything you do is secret from us, except your interminable conversations on the telephone. We don't know where you go or what you are doing half the time. You're never here except for meals, the place might as well be a hotel for all the time you spend in your home. And as for this boy, Sandy – are you serious about him?"

"Yes . . . No. I'm going away," I said making up my mind.

"Away? Away where?"

"I'm going abroad. I have my fare saved up, and the gold will be enough for my return fare. I'll get a job over there."

I had to go through all these explanations again when my stepfather came home, and I told Celia what I thought of her meddling and snooping. She had left the lid off my new nail polish too, and had borrowed my half-slip without asking.

We had a first-class row. Celia was in the wrong, but I was the one who ended up bursting into tears, rushing into my room and banging the door. I would have got a lock for it the very next day, but it was hardly worthwhile now I was leaving.

Twenty-Two

I decided to leave as soon as the university exams were over. My results were not likely to be good, as Mr Brill would surely fail me in his subjects and I hadn't done nearly enough reading in English Literature. Besides which, whenever something "important" in Mr Parfitt's book came up at the same time as a lecture, I had to cut the lecture.

He now called me in to tell me there would be less difficulty about time off for lectures next year, as I would be making up my own pages in my own time. The Women's Magazine was to be extended, and after Roma left I was to take over. It was, in fact, a promotion, he pointed out.

A red-hot flush of blood rose to the roots of my red hair. "I'm afraid I won't be here to take over," I said. "You see, I'm leaving."

The Chief of Staff, never very quick on the uptake, began to smile. "Eh?" he said.

"I'm leaving the *Standard*. I will not write any more rubbish for or about women. I am sick to death of women, and their pages, and their fashions, and their clubs and committees and associations. I'd rather write the

173

children's page at half the salary; I'd rather send out lilac and pink certificates to the tinies –"

"Er, well, I didn't know you felt that way about it, Marigold. You see, Mr Perceval wants to make a big feature of the Magazine, switching it to Thursdays. Then you could start an Answers column, that's always good for circulation, and we want to build up Thursday's paper; it's a bad day for Advertising. Of course you'd have to write a few letters to yourself to begin with, till it got going –"

"Oh, NO!" I clutched my head. "Not advice to the lovelorn! I could not, could not bear it."

"Well you think about it. When Roma leaves next month you'll be the Editress, and your salary –"

"Will have to go to someone else, since I won't be here either. I've saved enough for my fare to London, and I'm off overseas."

Afterwards as I sat at my desk in a brown study, doodling on a piece of copy-paper with my new fountain-pen (of which I had already chewed the end), I was making curling J's and R's, capital letters I liked the shape of: Jerusalem, I wrote, and Jurisprudence. Resuscitation, Rejoinder, Reunion, Reunion in Vienna. And then, from a writing-lesson remembered from kindergarten days, "Blessed are the pure in heart, for they shall see God." The inked words appearing on the smooth clean paper gave me, as always, a feeling of power and contentment.

Malcolm Marchant paused by my desk on his way out. He studied the copy-paper.

"I'd like the author of *Psychopathia Sexualis* to see your doodlings, my child," he said, smiling toothily.

I was too taken aback even to resent his my-childing.

"Who was that tall young chap I saw you having dinner with the other night?" he asked. "Bit of an outdoor type, eh? Bronzed Australian, and all that."

I put a double sheet of paper in my typewriter and pointedly began to type.

"I am not going to discuss my private life with you," I said, resisting an impulse to tell him of my great decision, and remembering how scared I had been of him and his superior airs when I first arrived.

I went round to tell Roma my news, but she was out. I wanted someone in whom to confide. On an impulse I went and saw Kurt, the Finance editor – a Czech, who was the only non-Australian on the staff. Already I was mentally orientated towards Europe. We had drunk burgundy together at an AJA dinner and I liked him, but since he was at least forty it was a kind of filial affection. He was *simpatico*.

"This is great news, Marigold!" he cried, sweeping some proofs off a chair so I could sit down. "Of course you must go. And you will be able to visit the beautiful city of Prague."

His large eyes glowed through their horn-rimmed glasses. His enthusiasm was infectious, but Prague was a place I had not thought of going to. What was there to see in Prague?

Kurt was shocked.

"First there is the Ultava, the legend-haunted Ultava; I would not exchange this ancient river for the Danube, the Seine and the Loire all rolled together."

Something of scepticism must have shown in my face – who had ever heard of the Ultava? – for he said challengingly, "You have heard of Bohemia?"

"Yes. My mother has some Bohemian glass."

"Well, Boehmia-Moravia is the old name for Czechoslovakia. You think it is a new country, but it is old, old as history."

I perceived that Kurt was wound up, so I let him run on, though Czechoslovakia didn't appeal to me. For one thing, I couldn't spell it.

"Why don't they call it Bohemia still?" I asked. "Czechoslovakia is such a mouthful."

Kurt looked offended. "The Slovenes would not have

liked that. It was the best name," he said. His eyes grew dreamy behind their horn-rims. "Nowhere on earth is such a mass of creative art to be seen in one city as in Prague."

"All right, I want to go there. It sounds very civilised."

"There is natural beauty, too, in the bends of the river, the parks of the Chateaux . . . You remind me a little of the *Diana* in Létna Park."

This sudden descent to the personal confused me, and I blushed, which made me furious. "Queen and Huntress, chaste and fair" – no, it didn't suit me at all. Large and hypnotic, Kurt's eyes were fixed on me appraisingly.

"And a little, also, of the deer about the pedestal, those slender creatures poised for flight. Yes, you have the eyes of a doe, at times; and at times also they have a wicked sparkle."

"As long as I don't look like a flying-ant," I said.

"An *ant*? But of course not. By the time you are thirty-five you will be a most attractive woman."

"Thirty-five! But I'll be *old*!"

He smiled tolerantly.

"You'll be surprised, my dear. Time has a way of expanding in front of us. It is like walking down an avenue which seems to end in a perspective point; but when you get to this point it has opened out, and there is a new stretch of road to travel. You will see." He nodded confidently.

A whole new road! Certainly my father had been forty-eight before he began his new life which had started with his supposed death. "And what about death?" I said aloud.

He shrugged his shoulders. "Who knows? Perhaps the avenue ends in a blank wall, after all. Or perhaps it takes a sharp turn, and a whole new vista appears. It is a mystery, and this makes life more interesting. Who would wish to work out a difficult puzzle, if the end is already known?"

"You're changing the metaphor," I said. "And I must let you get back to work."

"And when you are drinking coffee in the Café Fénix, looking down into the streets of Prague, think of me."

I promised that I would.

Next day I found a shipping agent and booked a berth tourist class on a liner leaving in four weeks for Marseilles; it was the off-season and fares were cheap.

Walking back to the office I played a game I had invented on trips to the city as a child. As each member of the crowd passed, I imagined a coloured thread extending back from his person to the home he had left: an invisible, non-tangling thread that wove and wound through the streets, in and out of the other people's threads, to make a coloured web.

I crossed and re-crossed the broad footpath, absorbed in the game. A heavy-faced woman – navy blue – dragging a small girl – pale green – crossed the paths of a purple youth and a buttercup-yellow girl. I went between them so that my own thread, which I imagined to be of a warm orange colour, became interwoven with theirs; and was tripped over by a hurrying businessman – dark grey – who glared angrily.

At the last corner I stopped to look down past the War Memorial to the twin spires of St Peter's Cathedral, above which towered a huge white cloud, solid as a marble monument.

I longed for Venetian palazzos and Roman fountains, and ruins, ancient and ivy-covered. All was too raw, too new; and in the sunbaked streets there was not a single fountain, save for a piddling thing that was turned off as often as not, to save power.

The streets were all straight, the whole thing was flat as a gridiron and nearly as hot. Two leafy avenues and a few green squares broke up the sterile pattern, but if a tree dared to grow too big some envious bureaucrat would cut it down, and plant a bed of petunias in its place.

The huge old gum trees which had once covered these plains in parklike profusion, had been cut down in the early days for firewood. The few left behind were now being rapidly removed to make room for electric power poles.

Perhaps they would be happy when it had all been reduced to one enormous, neat suburb, with every wild thing pushed back beyond the range of hills.

Roma and I celebrated at the South after work. I felt much older than when we had gone there with Jed Ryan, who meanwhile had joined a Sydney newspaper. I ordered a brandy cruster.

"To Europe!" said Roma, toasting me in Campari and soda.

"Prosit!"

We clinked glasses. I tried to feel festive, but I was sad about leaving Sandy and losing Roma. About leaving the *Standard* I had no regrets.

"We should really have a bottle of champagne," said Roma.

"But I don't really feel celebratory. I'm just glad I'll be leaving the office soon after you go. I won't be able to bear it without you, Stan." (I cannot *bear* it! was one of the dramatic phrases with which I annoyed my parents.)

"Thanks, Mal. I'll miss you too."

"I suppose you'll go and get married in Melbourne."

She smiled. "I might, who knows? I don't have your horror of the married state. My sister has two little boys, and she's very happy."

"You mean you're an *aunt*!"

My idea of an aunt was based on someone like Aunt Flora, or Uncle Fred's widow with the lilac hair. I was quite shocked.

We each had another drink, and by the time we left I

178

was feeling better. I was going to miss Strawberry too, I realised as I drove towards the gold-grassed hills, seeming to give out light as they reflected the western sky. I would certainly come back broke and unable to afford a car. I mentally took farewell of those close and friendly hills, which seemed to curve their arms about the city on the plain.

Twenty-Three

There was the usual presentation when I left the office. I would gladly have forgone this, knowing how everyone groaned "What, again?" when asked to contribute. However I received gratefully a useful and pretty travelling clock, and listened to Mr Smythe's jocular remarks about my supposed future career in Fleet Street.

I went round to Myfanwy's room afterwards to say goodbye – Roma had already left two weeks before, and the office was only half bearable without her. Myfanwy was alone sitting at her desk, thinking, with the smoke from her cigarette, clamped as usual in its holder between her strong teeth, curling about her short-cropped hair.

She nodded at me approvingly. "They haven't got you in with this marriage business, I see!"

"No fear. When does Helen leave?"

"In another month. This new girl she's supposed to be training is hopeless, and Helen's not much better, she's in such a broody state. Wish we had you back, even if you did leave banana-skins in the wastepaper basket. At least you could write out a Social Note without five spelling mistakes."

I grinned. "Did you notice that Mr Smythe, our friendly Associate Editor, forgot to mention how 'we are just one big, happy family'? Forgetting of course Ron Dickson, who was put off last month with three weeks' notice and a family of his own to support."

"Yes, the bastards! It would be a damn sight happier if Mr Smythe would accidentally impale himself on a copy-spike."

Myfanwy thoroughly approved of my going abroad, and so of course did Kurt, who had kissed my hand with European gallantry and presented me with a small volume of *Views of Ancient Prague*.

Sandy, of course, disapproved strongly. He became sunk in gloom, sure I would marry "some bastard off the boat, or even some foreigner", and never come back. I promised him I wouldn't get married, and would come back in a year at the most; but I refused to wear a ring or be bound in any way but by my word.

We had an emotional farewell in which he called me heartless and a deserter, and I ended up reassuring him in the only way I knew, by letting him seal the bargain with a final act of possession. He had set his seal on me, and I knew that I would return.

A week later I stood in the stern of the *Orinoco*, watching the sunset colours fade from the sky. I was tearing up pages of the *Standard* and scattering them in the sparkling wake; destroying symbolically a part of my past. Gulls dived after the pieces, divining accurately that they were rubbish; but retired defeated since they were not edible.

Sandy had not come down to the ship to see me off. He said he couldn't stand it, watching the streamers breaking and the water widening between us inch by inch, and, final twist of the knife, the corny little band on the wharf playing *The Maori Farewell* as they always did at an overseas liner's departure.

Now I leant on the ship's smooth wooden rail and felt the vibration of the screws which carried me away from him with every turn. Suddenly I wanted to go back.

We had edged away from the wharf so quietly that I did not at first realise we were moving, until the streamers started to tauten. I had been glad when all but the passengers were ordered ashore, and Celia could no longer bounce on my bunk, nor my mother keep repeating her injunctions about getting enough to eat and not forgetting to write. All this family fussing embarrassed me in front of my cabin mates, who had eyed me warily as an unknown quantity. (They had joined the ship in Sydney, and felt like old inhabitants.)

My stepfather had been unexpectedly helpful, pressing a note into my hand on leaving "for little extras". He had also undertaken to sell Strawberry for me, if anyone was foolish enough to buy the thing, and to send me the money. I kissed him goodbye with more than usual warmth.

Even Mr Muecke had given me a little pocket guide to the art treasures of Europe.

I had been touched to find flowers in the cabin from Sandy, and a good luck telegram from Noel Richards.

When everyone was ashore who was going ashore, I had stood at the high rail and watched Celia darting about the wharf below, collecting the coloured streamers that blew and clung about people's feet. The band droned out on xylophone and accordion:

> Now . . . is . . . the . . . hour
> For us . . . to say . . . goodbye . . .

and I felt the usual lump in the throat at the finality of departure.

Celia was not such a bad kid really . . . Already made tolerant by distance, I realised that when she grew up a bit she would be all right. My parents looked smaller and older and pathetic somehow in the waning light. My stepfather cupped his hands about his mouth and shouted something I couldn't catch; I smiled and waved. Mother, suddenly discovering me among the crowd at the rail, waved back and blew a kiss.

Then the space of water widened, the great bulk of the ship had swung out, guided by tugs, as we headed for the open sea.

Now we were well out; the deck lifted and fell with the surge of the Southern Ocean.

I put my hand on the taffrail and felt the engine vibrating like a pulse of life beneath my fingers.

"Life, here I come!" I said, and lifted my head to the breeze. An albatross followed us, floating on unmoving wings, only its head turning occasionally from side to side to scan the water.

The glow of the city, the lines of shore-lights had been left far behind in the dusk. The stars were beginning to come out.

Back there beneath the lamps, I thought, those foolish flying-ants were busy biting off their own wings for the sake of the new generation. And so it would go on forever.